This book is dedicated to:

My family for being so supportive during the stress of writing editing and publishing.

My friends, for listening to me babble about my characters and their shenanigans as well as giving me all the feedback ever.

Special thanks go to my husband, John Akridge for this book's title and our friend Patrick Downend, for help locating the cover art.

My Discord and local writing groups for all of the feedback, help with scenes, and some of them, reading the entire draft.

Maël Balland for the beautiful cover art from Pexels.

Egyptian Entanglement by Christine Akridge

Published by Christine Akridge

Copyright © 2023 Christine Akridge

Cover by Christine Akridge with a photo by Maël Balland.

ISBN: 9798370027406 (print)

Printed in USA

This is a work of fiction. Names, characters, business, events and incidents are the products of the author's imagination. Any resemblance to actual persons, living or dead, or actual events is purely coincidental.

Chapter 1

Cal looks at the envelope sitting on her coffee table. She knows the contents without opening it. She leans forward, shifting on the edge of her seat. Gently and slowly opening it, Cal unfolds the letter inside. She takes a deep breath. The envelope drops back onto the table, as she holds tight to the papers inside. Green eyes scan the page, reading what she already knows is there.

The judge has granted an uncontested divorce. Wolf hadn't even tried to fight it. A clear sign, that shows her how he feels about her, about them. Cal keeps her things and Wolf keeps his, including the property in Wyoming. Cal gets her last name back; she smiles softly at that news. No more having to sign with *his* last name. She didn't detest the name, but she did detest the man it is attached to. Cal turns, wincing slightly. She still has a few aches and pains from their visit to California. The doctors say it's normal, but not being able to do her usual activities is far from usual for the adventurer.

Letting the letter drop onto the table, Cal carefully makes her way down the hall and toward the bathroom. She doesn't bother shutting the door, it's just her after all. Cal turns on the water, letting it get hot and steamy before she steps under the spray and lets it carry her cares down the drain. Absently, her fingers reach up and touch the small tattoo behind her ear. She takes a moment to scrub her hair and body. Her fingers linger on the raised scar that almost ended her life and ended the life of her son. She hastily rinses off, her eyes snapping open and the water getting shut off. The towel is yanked from the bar, and she scrubs her hair dry before wrapping the towel around herself. She doesn't bother with the mirror.

Since the day she was released from the hospital, Cal rarely looks at herself on any reflective surface. Cal grabs clothes at random, only giving enough of a care to make sure the colors at least match. She doesn't care about how she looks as she pulls on jeans and a loose-fitting tank top over a black sports bra. She shoves her feet into flip-flops because she can't be bothered with real shoes. Cal makes her way back to the living room.

This apartment has almost the same layout as the one she had moved out of, just in a different part of the complex. She had missed Albuquerque and is very glad to be home. It has been a big help in healing her soul. She grabs her purse, slinging it over her head and settling it across her shoulder. Cal winces as the weight of the revolver smacks her in the back. She still carries it, not that it had done any good in Los Angeles. She hadn't even been able to get to her gun. As if her physical and emotional scars weren't enough, Cal's wood-handled .38 bears a gouge in the butt from one of the bullets that had passed through her.

Grabbing her keys, Cal steps out onto the porch. She shuts and locks the door behind her before making her way down the stairs. A short walk down the sidewalk brings her to her Jeep. She stares at the vehicle as if she is seeing it for the first time. This has become common, finding herself somewhere and have no idea how she got there. Running her fingers through her still damp hair, Cal unlocks the car. Tugging the door open, she tosses her purse into the passenger seat before sliding into the driver's seat and pulling the door shut with a thunk. Cal takes a deep breath in an attempt to focus before she even attempts to drive anywhere.

The key is slid into the ignition, and she fires the Jeep up. Backing out of her space, she pulls out onto Figueroa. It's nice to be back in her old neighborhood. She pulls out onto Central Avenue and heads toward downtown. Albuquerque has done a lot to clean up the neighborhood like Nob Hill. Little boutique shops, art stores, music, and bookshops line the road. Cal is glad to see this area, formerly overrun with drug dealers and prostitutes, is now thriving.

Cal turns into the parking lot of the Frontier Restaurant. She parks the Jeep and kills the engine. Opening the door, she grabs her purse and steps out into the warm afternoon air. She crosses the pavement, taking a deep breath before stepping into the crowded restaurant. Settling her bag over her shoulder, she gets in line. Cal has never been one for crowds before the shooting, and afterward, it got worse. The loud voices assault her ears and almost send her running from the restaurant, but she forces herself to stay. The Frontier is right across the road from the University of New Mexico, so it's a favorite hangout for students and staff alike. Standing in line, Cal tries to focus on the menu and ignore the surrounding noise. It's hard, but at least she can focus long enough to decide what to order. Her stomach grumbles quietly.

Cal smiles softly at the cashier before ordering a burger and fries. She pays for the food, grabs her number and soda cup, then heads for the soda fountain. Cal fills the cup with root beer and finds a table in the corner away from most of the patrons. Setting her cup down, Cal walks over to the pickup counter as her number is called. She takes her tray back to her table, then sits at the table, making sure she can see most of the room, with her purse nestled against her on the bench just in case she needs to get her pistol.

Cal eats slowly, keeping a watchful eye on the door. She only pulls her eyes away from the door long enough to scan the room, then focuses back on the door. The fries are delicious, overdone, as always. The burger is perfect and filling. It's the first meal Cal can remember enjoying in its entirety, despite the compulsive people watching. *Maybe I'm getting back to normal, well normal for me,* Cal thinks. She watches the crowd, noting students and professors. The lunch crowd is thinning out and the noise level drops to a dull roar. Cal dumps her wrappers and soda cup in the trash, setting her tray on top of the can. She grabs her bag, fishing her keys out of it, and makes her way out the exit.

For the first time in what feels like forever, Cal takes a deep breath to savor the warm desert air. It's the start of chile roasting season, and the breeze brings hints of spicy smoke to her nose. She closes her eyes, the smell making her feel rejuvenated and alive. It's one of the many reasons Cal has returned home to Duke City.

She climbs into her Jeep and heads out on the freeway. Cal decides to head for her office, having no other plans for the day. She is sad that her old office was newly occupied when she returned, but she had found a less expensive place. Cal would prefer to be in the older part of the city, around the history, but she wasn't that lucky. The good thing about the new office is Wolf wouldn't just randomly show up. Parking her Jeep in the parking lot of the metal and glass monstrosity, which makes her feel like an unwelcome explorer, Cal grabs her bag before she climbs out of the SUV. The vehicle is locked before she walked into the building.

Stepping inside, she winces at the blast of the AC. A few steps bring her to the elevator, and she presses the Up button.

The only redeeming feature of this new office is the view. She steps into the elevator door, turns to face out into the lobby. Cal presses an unlabeled button. The ever-superstitious crew and architect had left the thirteenth-floor button unlabeled. Cal, never one to have such silly beliefs, rather enjoyed having an office so far up and on a mostly empty floor. While the lobby had beautiful stone floors, the hallways had plushy carpets. Cal steps out into the hallway, making her way to her office. She unlocks the door, opens it, and steps over the threshold. Her office has the same plush black carpet as the hallway and is almost wall to wall bookcases. It is smaller than her old office and doesn't have the smell of old books and dust. No, this space smells too sterile, too clean. Cal has routinely asked the cleaning crew to leave her office alone, but they never listen.

The door swings shut behind her, and she sets her purse on the floor next to her desk. A small laptop sits in the middle of a fancy leather ink blotter Brock had sent her. It looks out of place on her old military surplus desk. Cal sits in her chair, also military surplus, and looks over the bookshelves. Books filled two full sets of shelves, a third has two shelves of her journals, and a couple of shelves of what is left of her artifact collection. Most of it has been sold, first to pay for the move to Wyoming, then to pay for the divorce and move home. Cal plans to get back to work and rebuild her collection.

Cal opens the laptop lid, hitting the power button. After she got home, she had replaced the old tower and monitor with something more portable. It didn't leave the office often, but she had the option to work from home now as long as she didn't have meetings. She logs into the computer. The background loads. It's an image of her, William, and Bernd at some dinner in Germany. They are all smiling, with big beers in hand. Cal can't remember what they were celebrating.

She clicks on her email and hums to herself as she scrolls through the messages. Orion, a friend, and a wonderful source of information is looking for an update on her health. He may have a job for her. She responds to the email, letting him know she is cleared to work and to send over any information. The next email that catches her attention comes from an unrecognized email address and just says EGYPT in the subject line.

Curiosity killed the cat; Cal thinks as she opens the email. She reads through the contents. It's the typical job, to find an ankh with the eye of Horus in the middle. Of course, like most artifacts she is hired to find, it's rumored to be cursed. None of this phases Cal. The one thing that is almost a deal-breaker is a line that says that the rest of the team has been hired. The last time Cal didn't hire the whole team, artifacts were stolen. Mikhail Maximov, as the email is signed, includes information as to where to meet him and travel details to get her to Egypt to meet the rest of the team. There are no other names or even job titles given. For half a second, Cal almost declines the offer despite the pay being offered. However, the money is enough to sway her decision. An almost empty bank account will make the adventurer turn on her instincts almost every time.

Cal replies, letting Mikhail know that she will be there. Cal clicks through the last of the emails before starting a message to Maylin to set up a flight to Los Angeles. After thinking for a moment, she discards the message and decides to drive instead. Cal smiles, excited to be back to work. She has been cleared for work for more than a month but has only gone on a few easy digs, one of which she was accompanied by Brock. He said he wanted to make sure she was safe, Cal doubted that. Now she is back to being on her own and loving it.

Cal shuts her computer down and turns to look out the window. Her smile blossoms into a grin as she watches the city below her. The sun is high in the brilliant blue sky, with wispy clouds drifting lazily by. The genuinely happy smile feels foreign to her but in a good way. For the first time since she was shot, Cal feels like herself again.

While Cal sits in her high-rise office, a familiar truck is backed into a space out of sight of her window. The figure behind the driver's seat looks up at the building. He knows which office is hers and sees her old Jeep, so he knows she is here. Wolf could go up, knock on her door, and say hi or grab her and kiss her, but he values his life too much to pull a stunt like that.

A simple job has brought him to Albuquerque and gives him an excuse to check up on her. This is something he does each time he is in town, even if she doesn't know he is there. Their marriage had ended not with a bang, but with a whimper. Wolf had come home from one of his many trips and Cal's stuff was gone. On the island, she had left divorce papers, already signed by her. Wolf sighs, looking up at the building. *How can she enjoy being here?* Wolf wonders, looking from the building over the parking lot. Wolf's phone buzzes, he skims the text message then drops his phone back to his seat.

A quiet tapping on his window causes him to reach for his gun, startled. Wolf turns, seeing a man in a dark uniform. It takes a few seconds for Wolf to realize it's the rent-a-cop that patrols the lot. He rolls the window down, raising an eyebrow. Wolf doesn't speak, instead, he glowers and does his best to look intimidating.

"Can I help you?" The man asks. He is sure he has seen the driver before, but the truck isn't familiar to him.

"Nah. I was just leaving," Wolf says, turning his key in the ignition. The engine fires to life. Wolf rolls his window up. The security guard watches as the truck pulls out of the parking lot and disappears down the road. The man returns to his little go-cart and resumes his patrol. Cal comes out of the building, just as the truck turns onto the road, and climbs into her Jeep. She leaves the parking lot, pulling out onto the road. Ahead of her she sees a vaguely familiar truck but shrugs it off. Old Chevy trucks are popular in Albuquerque. Cal swears she faintly smells the tobacco-scented wax Wolf had used to try and cover the old truck smell she had adored. She shakes her head, knowing it's just her brain putting memories with the sight of the old truck. Cal turns her focus back to driving.

Singing along with her radio, the truck slips from her mind almost as soon as it's out of sight. She smiles to herself, tapping her hands on the steering wheel as she guides her Jeep down the freeway and toward her home. The doctors said she would have good days and bad days. This is the first good day she has had in weeks. Cal is paying attention to the road and traffic, but not the time. She finds herself parking in the lot behind her apartment.

Only William and Quilla know where she lives and where her new office is. Brock would visit her, but they never meet anywhere close to her place. Cal trusted William not to say anything to Wolf, but since Brock and Wolf still work together, she doesn't dare let him know. She doesn't want Brock offhandedly mentioning anything to her ex-husband. Cal climbs from the Jeep, and heads into her apartment, still humming to herself. Of course, she doesn't know that Wolf knows where she lives. He found that right after he found the office. Finding people is one of the things he is good at.

Cal lets herself into her apartment, shutting and locking the door behind her. She sets her purse on the second-hand blue couch and hangs her key from the hook next to the door. Tugging the fridge door open, she reaches in and retrieves a bottle of Corona. She pops the cap off using the edge of her countertop before she heads for her bedroom. As she walks, a long drink is taken from the bottle.

Mentally, she is already writing lists. She grabs a notebook, her journal, and pen from her bedside drawer. Cal makes her way back to her living room, then decides she is going to enjoy the small balcony. She steps outside, taking a deep breath before settling herself into a beat-up old rocking chair and setting her beer on the small glass top table. She opens the notebook to a blank page, heads the page with EGYPT SUPPLIES on each line below that she writes out items: ammunition, tent, sleeping bag, clothes, food, first aid. Every other item, she sips her beer. Next to items like the tent and food, she writes question marks, making a note to email Mr. Maximov about those items.

November 9th

I am back to work! I'll be heading for Egypt. It is a supposedly haunted or cursed pendant. A gold Ankh with the eye of Horus in the middle of it. The organizer has hired the rest of the team, which I'm not sure how I feel about. I usually hire people I trust. The last time I didn't hire people I trusted, well, artifacts got stolen. He didn't even give me a list of positions he hired. I don't know if I have a rigger, or a medic, or what. I *hate* that. I am walking into this job blind, which is not a good thing when we will be out in the desert, and who knows how far from civilization.

Today was a good day. I managed to get through a whole meal at the Frontier without having a meltdown or leaving. I smiled, a real smile today. It felt so good. Maybe it's the smell of chile in the air, or maybe it's the job, but I think the good days are going to outnumber the bad. At least, I hope they are. The office was even enjoyable. It smells like that gross cleaner the staff uses. I need to figure out a way to mask that smell. It reminds me of a doctor's office.

I need to get out of this funk. I saw a truck like Wolf's today. For just a moment, I swore I smelled that same tobacco-scented wax he kept under the seat. That hurt a bit, but it didn't send me spiraling, so I am going to take that as a win. Just a few weeks ago, it would have.

I gotta get lists done for this trip and email Mr. Maximov about a few questions I have.

-Cal

Chapter 2

While Cal is sitting on her balcony writing lists and writing in her journal, Wolf is sitting in the back parking lot of The Roadie, one of Albuquerque's older theaters. It's small but serviceable. Since his last job here, there have been some upgrades to the doors, and from what he can hear, the sound system. Wolf opens the door to his truck and slides out of the cab of his truck. He pulls his shoulder holster out from behind the seat and slides his arms into it. There are minute adjustments made, so it fits snuggly over his t-shirt. The seat is snapped back into place, and he pulls the pistol box out from under the seat. Unlocking the box, Wolf carefully lifts his 10 mm pistol out of it and slides into the holster before the box is shut and locked again. He returns the box to its space under the seat and tugs on his shirt.

Wolf locks the truck and crosses the parking lot as he heads for the back door. The short, squat building remind him of better times, like so many other places in Albuquerque. Cal and he had come here to see a few concerts. Rock concerts where his lady had led the way through the crowd to the front row on many occasions. He wants to go see Cal and say he is sorry. Wolf knows she won't accept the apology, but he wants to put it all out in the open between them. He wants to tell her how he feels. Wolf lets himself in the backdoor, walking toward the stage. *Security for a concert, have I sunk this low?* He thinks with a sigh. At the front of the group stands a tall, dark-haired man. Dominik Paine is the theater manager for The Roadie and keeps the theater running smoothly.

Wolf only half listens to the conversation. He knows where he will be, at the back door he had just come through. Wolf lets his eyes travel the space. Two sets of double doors are directly across from the stage. In just a couple of hours, those doors would let in throngs of fans, letting them flow into the tiered platforms that formerly held theater seats. Dominik is finishing up assigning locations to the other bodyguards.

"Ok guys, grab your headsets and walkies. Set up will be starting in five minutes and the fans are already lining up outside." Dominik motions to the table just offstage left before he disappears backstage. Wolf strides over to the table, snatching up the walkie-talkie and headset. The walkie gets clipped to his belt and the earpiece is slid into his ear. The cable is slid down the back of his shirt, and under one strap on the holster to hold it in place, before he plugs it into the walkie-talkie. He takes his seat on a barstool by the back door.

He wonders if Cal will be here. She loves charity and the Gin Blossoms. There is no way she can say no to this. Maybe they would casually run into each other after the show, then he can invite her to dinner or out for drinks. Dominik is doing channel checks as he walks across the backstage area. Wolf waves him over, pulling his phone out of his pocket.

"Whatcha need Wolf?" Dominik asks as he joins Wolf by the back door.

"If you see this woman, can you please let me know?" Wolf turns his phone around so his temporary boss can see the screen. On it is a picture of Cal, taken between their wedding and the trip to L.A. She is dressed in jeans, and a tank top, sporting a small baby bump. She had just started to show when Wolf had taken the photo.

"Why? Are you in some trouble? She's looking for child support?" Dominik smirks, looking from the phone to Wolf and back again.

"Nah. Ex-wife. She lives in the city, and we probably shouldn't see each other." Wolf doesn't care to elaborate and does his best to keep the hurt from his eyes at the idea of child support. Dominik just nods. If the man notices the slightest flicker of sadness, he doesn't say anything.

"I'll keep an eye out," Dominik says. As he opens his mouth to say something, a voice crackles over the earpieces.

"Dominik, we need you at the box office." The voice says, tersely. Wolf raises his hand as if to say he gets it. Dominik strides off, and Wolf turns his full attention back to the door.

During all of this, Cal has made her list and emailed Mikhail about the camping supplies. She has even gotten some of her gear packed in her old climbing bag. Quilla has texted her, letting Cal know they are checked into the hotel, and she would be on her way soon. Cal is excited to spend time with her friend. The two of them are meeting up for dinner and drinks, just like in the old days. Cal gathers her things, heading inside to change. She sets the empty beer bottle and notepad on her table before returning the journal to her bedside table. Cal rummages in a tote of bathroom items, finally finding her makeup. She looks down at the cosmetics, then takes a deep breath and starts with her eye shadow.

Once her makeup is done, she heads into the bedroom. She digs through her closet, not sure what to wear for this outing. After much indecision, she settles on a pair of snug blue boot cut jeans with rhinestone-covered back pockets. For a blouse, she decides on a dark gray semi sparkly top with a deep V-neck. She sets aside her hiking boots, her usual go-to shoes, for a pair of chunk heeled combat boots. Finally, she takes the small dragon pendant off the wall and fastens it around her neck. She runs a brush through her hair, smoothing it down. Cal looks at herself in the mirror, feeling impressed.

There is a knock at the door, Cal jogs out into the living room. She looks through the peephole and pulls the door open.

Quilla smiles at her friend, looking over the girl. Cal waves her in.

"Chica! You look muy hermosa!" Quilla exclaims. She is dressed in western boots, a pair of dark blue boot cut jeans, and a simple black tank top under a plaid shirt. Cal blushes faintly, tucking a strand of hair behind her ear.

"Thanks, Quil. Been a while figured why the hell not," She slides the pistol from her purse, tucking it into a lockbox on her bookshelf. She smiles, sliding the bag over her shoulder. "David is ok with us going out?"

"Yeah. He knows we need this. And knows we're not as wild as we were in college," Quilla tosses the long braid over her shoulder as the two step out the door. Cal locks her front door, and the two friends make their way down the stairs, and toward her SUV. Quilla unlocks the car doors with a remote and climbs into the passenger seat. Cal slips into the passenger seat, buckling her seat belt.

"Where're we headed?" Cal asks.

"Figured we'd hit the art fight at Tractor Brewing Company, and we got you a little present," Quilla says, pulling two tickets from the center console and handing them to her friend. "Drinks, and a show."

"You guys didn't have to do that, Quil," Cal says, looking at the Gin Blossoms tickets. Cal returns them to the console as

Quilla backs out of the space and guides the small SUV through traffic to the bar. They pull into the parking lot, and the two women step out. Quilla smooths her shirt down and adjusts her jeans ever so slightly. Cal just rakes her fingers through her hair and takes a deep breath.

She follows Quilla into the bar, which is noisy and warm, bordering on hot. Cal looks around, suddenly panicking. It feels like there are too many people in here and the space is too small. Quilla guides her friend to a table in the corner, where they can see both the bar and the artists. Cal takes a seat with her back to the wall, watching the room. The artists are set up on a stage, where both they and their pieces are visible. Quilla walks up to the bar to order drinks.

Quilla returns to the table, pressing a cold Corona into her hand. Cal wraps her fingers around the bottle, bringing it to her lips and taking a long drink. She closes her eyes, letting the beer fizz its way down her throat. Slowly the bottle is lowered to the table and Cal sighs again. Quilla settles herself into a chair next to her.

"You ok?" Quilla asks, trying to keep her voice quiet but also be heard over the din of the restaurant.

"Yeah, just panicked a bit. Large crowd, and a lot of noise," she doesn't add anymore, just vaguely gestures to herself and the crowd. Quilla nods. She had missed the chaos in China and after the Las Vegas baby show, she had been on a flight back to Texas to return to her university and professional tour circuit. She was lecturing on the ruins they had found in Peru, Wolf's first dig with them, and only knew vague details about the loss of half their team in China and a few details of the shooting in Los Angeles. Quilla wants to help, but she knows that pushing Cal will get her nowhere.

The two friends settled into idle chit-chat, sipping their beers and watching the artists as they paint and draw. Around them, people talk and cheer on their favorite artist. On the stage, the artists joke with each other. Cal watches and listens, drinking her beer. She is amazed by how talented the artists are. She could sketch small, simple things, but nothing like what these wonderful people were doing on stage in front of a large crowd.

The time ticks by, and just as the art auction is starting, the two ladies leave the restaurant. Quilla unlocks the car and the two climb into their seats. The car starts and Quilla backs out of the space. She drives from the restaurant toward The Roadie. They turned the music on, singing along with the radio as they drive down the road.

The parking lot of The Roadie is already busy. People in bright orange vests are directing traffic. Quilla mutters under her breath, swearing in Spanish, as the cars creep along through the rows of vehicles. When she finds the first free space, Quilla pulls into it, throwing the SUV into park. Cal can't help but giggle at her friend. Cal grabs the tickets and steps from the vehicle. Quilla climbs from the car. They both take a moment to tuck their IDs and money in their pockets before the car is locked up. The two head for the doors, and the long line of fans waiting to get in.

It feels like forever in the shuffling line before they get inside. The last concert Cal had seen here was in high school. Quilla moves behind Cal, letting her push her way to the front of the crowd. Quilla moves to stand next to her friend at the barricade. The roadies for the openers are making final adjustments to the setup, tuning guitars, and doing sound checks. Cal smiles. She leans against the railing, watching the men and women on stage.

Behind the curtains, sits Wolf. Dominik is directing traffic backstage and trying to keep everyone happy. Wolf shifts on his barstool, already eager for the night to be over and to get paid. He would return to his hotel for the night, then it would be back on the road to Maine for a brief visit with his family. Dominik makes his way over to Wolf.

"Can you take a spot at the front? We just had a guy walk-off," Dominik says. Wolf motions to his shirt.

"Even armed?" Wolf asks. Dominik nods, then walks off to deal with another issue in the theater. Wolf stands and makes his way to the front of the stage, standing at one end. Toward the center of the barricade, he spots Quilla first, then

Cal. He stands his ground, reminding himself that he is here to do a job. *At least now I know she is safe;* he clenches his fist as the opening band takes the stage. The music isn't half bad, and Wolf finds himself tapping his foot to the beat.

Quilla and Cal tap their hands on the railing, watching the local band. The room is too crowded, and Cal doesn't like the feeling of the wall of people at her back. Her anxiety flares up before she can stomp it back down. She isn't sure how long she can keep this in check, and it must show on her face. Quilla gives her a gentle nudge.

"You ok?" Quilla asks as the music quiet and the fans cheer around them.

"Yeah, I'm good," Cal replies, with what she hopes passes for a real and confident smile.

"If it gets too bad, let me know, and we will leave," Quilla assures her friend, patting her arm. The house lights come up part way as the set is changed for the Gin Blossoms. Some people head out to the concession and merchandise stands, while others head outside to have a smoke. Cal shifts her weight from one foot to the other as she watches the various techs change out instruments and stage dressing. Someone, reeking of beer and much larger than Cal, catches her in the back with an elbow. Cal turns, one hand closing into a fist as she pulls back, fully intent on beating the crap out of whoever just elbowed her. A firm hand closes around her wrist. It's larger than Quilla's. Cal spins to see who had the balls to grab her. Security steps forward, watching Cal and her friend intently. There is Wolf, smiling that damn crooked grin that still sends butterflies swirling in her stomach.

"Do you have to get into a fight on my watch?" He asks. "Good to see you taking care of yourself," he says as he lets go of her wrist and looks her over.

"Don't worry about me, Wolf. Not your job anymore," she says through clenched teeth. Cal turns to face the barricade again, her hands wrapping around the metal bar and squeezing until her knuckles turn white. "If I ever see you again, I'll shoot you, Bryan." She stares at the stage, ignoring Wolf, who returns to his spot at the end of the stage. Quilla rests her hand on Cal's forearm until she sees her friend visibly relax, and then she allows her hand to drop away.

"Do you want to leave?" Quilla asks, glancing at Wolf then back to her friend.

"No, I'll be fine. Just wasn't expecting him to be here," Cal says as she closes her eyes and takes a long deep breath, trying to slow her heart rate. When her eyes open, she looks calmer and feels so too. Quilla still keeps an eye on her friend, worried. The crowd behind them is filing in as the Gin Blossom's techs are finishing the soundcheck.

"We can go if this is too much," Quilla says again as the music starts. Cal shakes her head, determined to make it through the full set. Quilla and her husband were so nice for getting tickets to this show. There is no way she is letting them go to waste. The band bounces from newer stuff to their older hits and back again. After the first two or three songs, the friends find themselves singing along. Cal relaxes, despite the ever-watchful eyes of Wolf. Occasionally, their eyes would meet, but both would look hastily away. The band closes with *Hey Jealousy*, which Cal and Quilla sing at the top of their lungs.

Wolf, once again, finds himself tapping his foot to the beat. In his pocket, his phone buzzes, but he barely notices, focusing on the hustle and bustle that comes with the concert ending. As the band is shuffling back to their dressing room, the house lights come up. Wolf watches as Cal and Quilla leave, then returns to his seat by the back door. He takes a moment to look at his phone, finding an email with the subject line EGYPT. Opening the message, Wolf scans it. The email lists facts about an ancient pendant a rich Russian wants for his collection. Wolf doesn't care about the history but does care about the payment. There is a note stating that the team has been hired, but there are no names. Wolf replies to the email, letting the man know he will take the job. Despite the time difference, Mr. Maximov replies promptly with travel details. Wolf has three days to get his stuff together and meet this man in Los Angeles.

It's a shuffling and jostling walk back to the car, but Quilla and Cal finally make it to the SUV. The doors are unlocked, and two friends spill into the seats. They sit for a moment, with the doors closed and their ears ringing. The radio is turned down once Quilla starts the car and heads back toward the freeway. She isn't sure if she should ask Cal about Wolf or leave it be. They ride along in silence until Cal speaks.

"Did I tell you I got a dig?" She keeps her voice nonchalant as she speaks.

"No! When? Where?" Quilla squeaks, glancing at her friend for just a second before pulling her eyes back to the road.

"I'm leaving in three days to go to LA to meet with the buyer and organizer. Some Russian guy then I'm heading to Egypt to look for an ankh pendant," as Cal speaks, she watches the murals alongside the freeway speed by.

"Have you told Brock? Did you get a team hired yet?" The last questions flow together with excitement.

"Team has already been hired," Cal shrugs. "The organizer took care of that." Cal chews nervously on her lower lip. "Honestly, I'm nervous about returning to LA, and nervous about not hiring my team."

"Have you been back since…" Quilla lets the words die off before she finishes her sentence.

"No, and I hadn't planned to," she is not ready to return to the city where she almost died, but she needs to work. Her bank account is getting low, and she is starting to get a little stircrazy.

"Promise me you will be careful, chica," Quilla says as she guides the car off the freeway and toward Cal's apartment. "Promesa," she repeats, more forcefully.

"I promise." Cal forces a smile as they pull into the parking lot of the apartment. "You wanna come in and have a beer?"

"I can't. David is waiting for me back at the hotel," Quilla laughs. "He didn't want to intrude on girls' night."

"Tell him I said Hey," she shakes her head, climbing out of the vehicle. She checks for her wallet, and keys before waving to her friend. Quilla waits until Cal is safely inside, and her lights are on, before she makes her way out of the parking lot and back toward her hotel.

Cal tucks her wallet and keys back into her purse. She sets the bag on her kitchen table. After making sure the door is locked, and the lights are off, Cal makes her way down the hall. She kicks her boots off and strips out of her concert clothes. Grabbing a makeup wipe, she takes one last look at herself in the mirror before scrubbing her makeup off. Once her face is clean, Cal goes into her bedroom. She digs out a pair of loose-fitting basketball shorts and a tank top from one of her dresser drawers and gets dressed. Cal tosses her clothes in the hamper. She writes a short journal entry, then climbs under her big fluffy comforter. As she dozes off to sleep, she hums *Hey Jealousy*. She hardly makes it to the chorus before she is asleep.

Wolf makes sure he has cleared the backstage area and collects his pay. As he makes his way to his truck, the money is slid into his wallet. He unlocks his truck, sliding onto the seat. He starts the truck up and pulls out onto the road. Wolf cruises around the city aimlessly for some time. He isn't ready for sleep yet. Wolf finds himself driving by some of her old haunts. He drives past the museum, her old office, and the little Mexican restaurant where they shared many meals. After this painful reminder, he turns his vehicle back toward the freeway, which is mostly empty at this late hour. He takes a long detour back to the hotel, driving through the parking lot of her apartment complex. He pauses in the parking lot, behind her Jeep, and looks up at her windows. The lights click off, and this satisfies his need to know she got home safe, so he turns the truck back out onto the road and the freeway. Once he is back at his hotel and settled in for the night, he isn't awake for long.

The next morning and the day after are busy. Cal leaves a day earlier than she needs to drive to California. Wolf drives to Denver for a two-day dig and then drives to California. This is the first time either of them has returned to LA since Cal was shot. While they are staying at the same hotel, Cal and Wolf manage to miss each other at check-in and their rooms are at the opposite ends of the hotel.

November 10th

Quilla and I went out for girl's night. David and she are in town on a vacation. I am glad her man is ok with us taking off, especially since he remembers how we were in college. It was supposed to just be dinner and drinks, but they surprised me with tickets to Gin Blossoms.

It was all fun and games until Wolf showed up. I guess he was working security. I got elbowed, and almost punched out the guy who elbowed me. Wolf grabbed my arm to keep me from punching the guy. I threatened to shoot him the next time I saw him. It was a stressful situation made worse but I made it through the rest of the concert. I am surprised that security didn't escort us out.

The concert was amazing. I am so glad I got to go. Now sleep. I gotta get stuff together tomorrow. I am going to drive to California instead of flying, so I am going to leave early.

-Cal

November 13th

Gear is packed, and Jeep is loaded. I don't need to bring a tent or anything as that has been provided. Short entry. More tomorrow.

Chapter 3

"What the fuck are you doing here? I thought I said I'd shoot you the next time I saw you!" Cal snaps. Her eyes focus on the familiar shape sitting at the table. Her hands fumble for guns she knows aren't there. Wolf locks eyes with her, and the last eight months come flowing back.

In his mind, he sees Cal laying in the hospital bed, William by her side. She was fighting for her life. The doctor's words are still strong. Rhory, their son, hadn't made it. Cal was barely holding on. William had joined them as soon as he got the news. Her supposed friend, Zenaida, had taken off before the cops showed up, dumping Cal's purchases in the parking lot as she sped off. Wolf and Brock had killed one of the shooters and wounded the other. They had given the police all the information they had. Rhory's things had been put into his nursery and his room boarded up. Brock and William had cared for the healing archaeologist, while Wolf threw himself into finding the people who had done this. He had wanted to avenge his son and his wife.

Ex-wife, he corrects himself. Cal survived and seemed to be stronger than ever. Their marriage had not. As soon as she could, Cal was back on digs. She buried herself in travel and jobs. Wolf was always gone, tracking down drug dealers and the like. When they were home at the same time, they fought. There were not just small fights, but full-blown screaming matches that usually ended in one of them leaving either to stay in town or down at William's. Wolf had returned from one of his trips to find her things gone and divorce papers on the island. His last gift to her had been an uncontested divorce. William was able to keep his cabin, and both friends kept in touch with him. They just don't visit him in Wyoming. It's too painful.

"What the fuck are you doing here?" Cal repeats through clenched teeth, standing next to the table now. Wolf is the last person she wants to see. He blinks, her words ripping him back to the present rather abruptly.

"I got called for a job. What're you doing here?" He asks, words clipped and terse.

"Same." She replies. Her eyes narrow as she sits across from him. *Where is the buyer?* Cal wants to leave. No job is worth putting up with Wolf.

"Dr. Coburn? Mr. Corrigan?" A portly fellow in a white suit jacket approaches the table. His bald head shines in the low restaurant lights. Wolf's gut twists at the use of Cal's maiden name. The man's Russian accent is thick but understandable.

"Yes. You must be Mikhail Maksimov," Cal's voice turns polite and professional. A tone of voice she only uses for business meetings. Wolf just looks from the man to Cal and back again.

"It is a pleasure." He motions Wolf over so he can sit down. Reluctantly, Wolf slides closer to Cal, but still tries to keep his distance. "If I remember, you two are already acquainted, correct?"

"You could say that," Wolf quips. Cal glares at him.

"Ah, well then," the man pauses. "Hopefully that will not be a problem."

Cal opens her mouth to protest, then stops. She takes a deep breath and replies, "not a problem." She needs to keep in mind the payday. Her bank account is dwindling. Besides, they had worked well together in the past, of course, that had been before everything. Wolf nods, momentarily looking hesitant.

"Good." The man nods, pulling an envelope from the inside pocket of his coat. Cal grabs it before Wolf has a chance. She pulls out the folded papers, gently unfolding them. The stack contains translated legends, drawings, and descriptions, all the usual information needed for this sort of job. Cal unfolds the map, making a mental note to roll it back up.

"I think you will find everything you need," Mikhail says. Wolf picks up a drawing of the artifact, a simple ankh-shaped pendant with the Eye of Horus in the middle. Not an uncommon image to find.

"Everything except half the payment. Half now and half on return, no matter the outcome. Remember?" Cal reminds the man. Wolf admires her blunt attitude. It's one of her better qualities.

"Ah yes," Mikhail feigns a lapse in memory, then produces two more envelopes from inside his jacket. Each envelope bears one of their names in neat block handwriting. He hands the envelopes over to them, allowing them to count the cash. "I have mailed out payments to the rest of the team already." Mikhail stands.

"Can I get a list of team members? Or jobs that were hired for?" She asks, looking at the bald Russian.

"My boss has asked me not to give that information out. Everyone had been vetted. There should be no issues." Mikhail says tersely. Cal narrows her eyes at the man.

"Not what I wanted to hear, but ok. Now we have everything. We'll be in touch," Cal stands, shaking the man's hand. It's sweaty. She pulls her hand back, fighting the urge to wipe it on her shorts. Wolf slides from the bench, also shaking their employer's hand. He has more tact than Cal and waits until the man has left to wipe his hand on his jeans. Cal strides toward the exit, leaving Wolf standing there admiring the view before shaking himself back to reality.

Those days are gone, he reminds himself before following her. It brings a small smile to his face to see her old Jeep parked next to the restaurant. "Hey, Cal!" He hollers, jogging after her. "You live locally or staying at a hotel?" He asks, pausing as she turns around. Wolf tries to keep out of her personal space. He knows she isn't living nearby, but doesn't want her to know that. At least not yet.

"What's it to you?" Cal asks, leaning on the front fender of the Jeep. Her eyes narrow at him as Wolf walks closer to her.

"I figured we should chat, prepare for this. We're going to be stuck at a campsite together, and trekking through a tomb," Wolf says, trying to at least mend the bridges they both had burned so many months ago. Cal stares at him, arms crossed over her stomach. Wolf offers her a friendly smile. She sighs, shaking her head. If she is feeling anything, her face stays stoic, however that smile has sent the butterflies in her stomach swirling.

"I'm staying at the La Quinta up the road," Cal says, regretting it but at the same time liking the idea of spending time with him. Despite how things ended, Cal still has many fond memories of their life.

"What a coincidence. So, am I," Wolf replies, "meet you there, or do you want to go grab dinner and drinks tonight?" He tips his head slightly, relaxing a bit as they talk.

"No drinks, Wolf. That is how we ended up here. Meet you at the hotel, we can talk in the breakfast area," Cal says, forcing distance between them by walking around the front of the Jeep and pulling the door open. Wolf watches as she climbs in and fires the vehicle up. He moves back to the sidewalk, watching Cal drive off. He stares after her, then turns to his vehicle. Wolf climbs into his truck, gathering his thoughts before starting his vehicle and heading toward the hotel. Once there, he parks next to her Jeep.

For a few minutes, he lets all the fond memories come flooding back: the move to Wyoming, the road trips, the sing-a-longs. There had been many hours of laughter in that old SUV. Wolf shakes his head to clear it, climbs from his truck, locks the door, and heads into the hotel.

Sitting in her room, Cal rests her head in her hands. She sighs. After a minute or two, when she is sure the tears will stay behind her eyes, she stands. Cal walks across the room, grabbing her journal off the table. She sits back down on the bed, picks up the hotel pen. The book is opened to a marked page, and she starts writing. The pen scratches across the paper as Cal writes quickly. The words scrawl angrily across the page. A single teardrop splashes to the page, making the ink run. She stops writing, looking down at the running ink. She sets the book and pen aside. Cal looks up, catching sight of herself in the mirror above the dresser, silent tears rolling down her face. She watches for a moment; unaware she had been crying. Cal wipes her face with the back of her hand.

After eight months, seeing Wolf should have been easier on her. He made his decisions and she made hers. Fresh tears prickle at her eyes, threatening to spill down her cheeks. Cal clenches her hand tightly, taking a few deep breaths. The palms of her hands burn as she opens them. She looks down, finding deep crescent shapes dug into the palm of her hand. Cal stands, taking another deep breath to calm nerves as she grabs her wallet, room key, and her cellphone.

Time to go face the ex, she thinks as she leaves the room and heads down to the breakfast room. She stops in the hallway, listening to the door click shut behind her. *One foot in front of the other. Stay calm. Don't kill him.* Cal thinks repeatedly as she makes her way down the hallway and across the main office. Cal comes to a complete stop in the doorway to the breakfast room. She tries to force herself forward, but can't seem to get her feet moving. Straight ahead of her, sitting in one of the horseshoe-shaped tables with a half wall, sits Wolf. She can see the top of his head and knows he is looking toward the doorway. Those intense dark eyes would be taking in their surroundings, on the lookout for trouble. She has always imagined their son would have had those same deep brown, bordering on black, eyes.

Another deep breath comes out as a shuddering sigh, and she can finally get her feet moving again. Cal crosses the breakfast area. Before reaching Wolf and the table, Cal pulls herself up straight and puts on a brave face. She slides into the seat, across from him. Cal folds her hands, with the left one over the right. The two of them sit silently. She doesn't look directly at him, instead, her eyes focus on a spot just over his shoulder. Cal holds her jaw firm, trying not to let her emotions get the best of her. Tears and swear words threaten to spill forth in a torrent of anger as she fights to calm down.

"You wanted to talk?" Cal's words are short and clipped. Wolf blinks, pulling himself back to the present.

"Yeah. It's been a while since we saw each other," Wolf says as he shifts uncomfortably in his seat.

"You mean other than the concert," Cal says. Her eyes shift from the spot just over his shoulder to him. Her heart skips a beat, and it's like she is seeing him for the first time. Just like Peru, she finds herself lost in the dark abyss of his eyes. While he hasn't physically aged, he seems more mature than the angry boy she had left in Wyoming. Her gut twists. She pulls her attention back to the space over his shoulder.

"How ya been?" He finally asks. During their moment of silence, Wolf had been examining her as she had him. He notices her hair is longer, now hanging past her shoulders. Around her neck hangs the simple black cord with the peridot and silver dragon pendant shining in the lights. "Still wearing the dragon, I got for you, huh?" He adds, although he isn't sure why.

"Says the guy with a wedding ring tan line," Cal replies. The words come out sharper than she means for them too. Wolf looks down at his hand as if he is seeing the tan line for the first time.

"You want to talk about not letting go?" He reaches across the table, pulling her hand right out from under her left. On her right ring finger, shines the small diamond on her engagement ring and the wedding band.

She pulls her hand away, half glaring at him. Her skin feels too warm where he touched it. "It wasn't all bad, Bryan. I want to remember those good times."

"We did have a lot of those," Wolf mumbles. "But that all changed."

"Yeah, cause I fucked up," Cal grumbles. Wolf nods, there is no way he is going to deny that her need to give people second chances had been part of why they ended up here. She had screwed up. If Cal had listened to someone, and not given that drug dealing bitch a second chance, things would be different. They wouldn't be where they are now. Cal had wanted to believe Zenaida when she had said she was clean and no longer running in the crowds that had driven them apart their senior year of high school. Believing the woman had ruined the life Cal and Wolf were building.

"If you weren't so damn stubborn, Calamity, none of this would have happened." His words are sharp. Cal winces, turning her gaze to the tabletop. She turns her rings around her finger, fighting back tears. Wolf leans back in his seat, crossing his arms over his chest. A conceited smirk spreads across his face. He didn't like to hurt her, but it vindicated him that she knows he is right. She sighs and runs her fingers through her hair before she turns her soft jade-colored gaze to him.

"If you're just going to sit here and make me feel like shit, I'm leaving." As she speaks, Cal slides to the end of the bench.

"No. Stay," he raises his hand as if to stop her. "They didn't tell you who got hired, either huh?" Wolf adds, figuring now would be a good time to change the subject, and shop talk is always good. She had asked about it during the meeting, but he wasn't sure if she was clueless about the team or if that had been for his benefit.

"No. I didn't even know you were hired," she half snarls. Cal looks past him, still turning her rings around her finger.

The two fall into an almost suffocating silence before Wolf speaks again, "You gave up control? Who are you and what did you do with Calamity?"

"I didn't have a choice, Bryan." His given name is spat out as if it leaves a bad taste in her mouth. "He hired everyone before I even agreed to take the job." She adds, only slightly less rude this time.

"I wonder why..." Wolf pauses for a moment, "don't they usually let the lead pick their team members?" Cal nods. Once again, the silence is uncomfortable. The tension between the two is almost palpable. Wolf looks down at his hands, fingers running over the tan line where his band once sat. It's currently back in his room, tucked safely into his clean-up kit. Cal's eyes turn to her rings.

"How have you been, Wolf?" Cal finally asks, her voice just barely above a whisper.

"Not too bad. How about you?" As Wolf speaks, his voice sounds strange. She looks up at him, locking eyes with her former bodyguard. Normally flinty eyes have softened, showing genuine concern. The last time she saw that look was over the Atlantic, when he was worried that her pregnancy had been a cruel joke and that she was still working.

"Getting better," she replies with a small, almost timid smile.

"That's good. Any interesting finds recently?" He asks, figuring keeping the conversation on work was the best course of action right now. They will have plenty of time to talk over everything else once they are in the field.

"Not really." She shrugs. "Quilla is doing another tour with the Peru find. They finally got the whole site excavated."

"That's amazing." Wolf smiles. It's a bright, happy, genuine smile. The smile that had melted her heart and still gives her chills. He takes a deep breath then asks, "how are you healing?" He immediately turns his eyes away, knowing how sensitive of a subject he has touched on, but he wants to know.

"Good. The doctors say aside from some scar tissue, I'm perfectly healthy, well as healthy as a person who was shot and almost died can be," she shrugs. She is physically fine, but still refused to see any form of grief counselor.

"Good to hear. Was there a list of team members in all that information you snatched up?" Again, he changes the subject back to work. He wants to keep the conversation light and comfortable.

"Nothing. For all I know, we're it," she says with a smirk.

"Once upon a time, that would have been a perfect vacation." The words are out of his mouth before he can stop them. Cal narrows her eyes at him. She knows he is right. At one point, they would have celebrated a job with just the two of them. Those jobs had been few and far between, but they had happened.

"Yeah, sure," she mutters, then looks around the room. It's a brightly lit space with cream-colored walls. The seating is all dark brown with burnt, orange-colored pillows. Cal is not sure who chose the colors, but she is sure they're color-blind with this gross combination. She is no decorator, but even she can tell this looks terrible. "This is so damn awkward," she says with a quiet sigh.

"It's not easy. That's for sure," Wolf replies, tapping his fingers on the tabletop.

"Can we even do this?" Cal asks, turning her gaze back to Wolf.

"As long as it doesn't turn out like China," Wolf smirks. Cal's eyes narrow. Her gaze turns icy. Wolf winces, "Too soon?"

"Yeah. Too soon." Cal pulls her phone, checking the time. Her stomach growls quietly. She stands, tucking her phone back in her pocket. "I'm going to grab some dinner."

"Care for some company? I'll even drive." Wolf offers, slowly standing.

"I guess. It can't be any more uncomfortable than this," she says as she turns and walks toward the front door of the hotel. Wolf follows, fighting the urge to walk at her side as he had for years. "Which vehicle?" She says over her shoulder.

"We can take mine. I'm parked right next to you," Wolf replies, digging his keys out of his front pocket.

"Of course, you are," she grumbles, rolling her eyes.

"It's not like I did it on purpose. It's the first parking spot I saw," Wolf defends himself. He has parked there on purpose, just like he found out where her office is and her apartment. He still loves her and tells himself it's only because he wants to make sure she is safe. Everyone else says it looks like stalking.

Cal stands at the passenger door, tapping her foot as she impatiently waits for him to unlock the vehicle. Wolf unlocks the driver's door and climbs up into the cab of the truck. He cleans off the seat, sliding everything behind it, before he leans over and unlocks her door. She tugs the door open, pulling herself up into the cab. She sits in the passenger seat, buckling her seat belt. Before everything happened, she would have parked herself in the center seat to be close to him. Now she practically presses herself to the passenger door.

Wolf slides the key into the ignition and turns the truck on. He guides the truck out of the parking lot. They drive in almost total silence for a few miles, except the radio playing quietly.

"Any place in particular sound good?" Wolf asks, glancing at Cal out of the corner of his eye. She is staring out the window, watching the scenery.

"In and Out Burger," she mumbles quietly, watching businesses drift by but not seeing any of them. They pass stores and restaurants of all kinds as Wolf guides the truck through busy dinner-time traffic. They pass an Elephant Bar. It's not *the* Elephant Bar, but the sign is enough to send Cal's hands to her lower abdomen. Tears fill her eyes, threatening to spill down her cheeks. Wolf doesn't notice the reaction at first. He is too busy parking the truck. He turns to tell her they've arrived.

With one hand still resting on her lower stomach, Cal scrubs tears off her cheeks and from her eyes with the back of her hand. Her breathing is ragged, and she is fighting to get it under control. Before his brain can stop him, Wolf slides across the seat and wraps his arms around her. He pulls her close, guiding her head to rest just under his chin. Cal relaxes into him, feeling his warmth and taking in the smell of his skin. As always, it's a mix of a woodsy cologne and gunpowder. Ragged breaths smooth out, allowing her to focus on her surroundings. As her brain catches up to the situation, her body tenses in his arms. She pushes him away with one hand and fumbles the seatbelt off with the other. Once the seatbelt is off and the door is open, Cal practically jumps out of the truck. Wolf slides away, cursing under his breath. He watches as she glares at him from just outside the truck.

"Keep your damn hands off me, Bryan. You lost that privilege when you decided revenge was more important than your wife," Cal says through a clenched jaw before turning on her heel and striding into the small red, white and yellow building. Wolf sits in the truck, watching her in the rearview mirror. At that moment, his world just felt right. Whether she will admit it or not, hers did as well. He pulls himself out of the truck, jogging across the parking lot to catch up with her. Cal is already at the register, paying for their dinner.

"Thanks," he says quietly, lifting their tray as their number is called.

"You're welcome," she says coolly, walking toward a booth in the back. Cal is suddenly exhausted and is not ready to deal with whatever they had or may have. She feels panicked and scared. Cal wants to return to the safe space in his arms, listening to his heartbeat. *Come on Calamity. Get your shit together*. She thinks, grabbing her burger, fries, and milkshake off the tray. Cal takes a sip of the chocolate shake, sighing happily. As soon as she gets her hands to stop shaking, she lifts her burger and takes a large bite. Wolf's burger is already half-eaten, and his gaze is fixed on the tray. He doesn't dare look up at her. Cal eats slowly, managing to eat half her burger and most of her fries in the time Wolf has eaten his entire dinner. He sips his milkshake, eyes glancing around the loud and crowded restaurant. Cal pushes the food away, picking up her milkshake. "Ready to head back?" She mumbles quietly, looking down at her drink. She plans to go back to the hotel and lay down. Exhaustion has taken hold of her.

"Yeah, give me just a second," Wolf says, typing into his phone. A few more taps on the screen, and he tucks it into his pocket. Without another word, he clears the table and takes all the trash to the garbage can. They both grab their drinks and walk to Wolf's truck. He unlocks the door, pulling himself up into the driver's seat and setting the phone next to him. Cal wearily drags herself into the passenger seat, buckles up, and slouches against the door with both hands wrapped around the cup containing her extra thick chocolate milkshake. Cal sips her drink as they pull out of the parking lot.

Wolf reaches down, turning the volume up on the phone. Cal watches him, confused. The route he follows is longer, bypassing the Elephant Bar. Cal listens to the slightly British accented female voice guiding Wolf through the busy LA streets toward their hotel.

"Since when do you use a GPS?" Cal asks, her voice still quiet, but Wolf thinks he hears a giggle.

"Don't have a navigator, these days so I had to learn how to use bitch in a box," he motions toward the phone. Cal chuckles again, taking another drink from her cup. Wolf rolls his eyes at her as he guides the truck back into the parking lot. He parks in a space near the building, away from her Jeep. The two climb from the truck cab and lock their doors. Cal heads into the building, with Wolf following her. She stops in the lobby, turning to face him.

"It's been nice to hang out, Wolf. Even if you're still a pain in my ass," she offers him a small wave. "See ya at the airport tomorrow." Cal smiles at him, a real smile, before she walks down the hall. Wolf watches her, aching to follow her, but knows that is a bad idea.

Instead, he turns and walks to his room. He wasn't going to chase her as he had for so long. She would have to chase him if she wanted to make things work, even on just a professional level. Wolf's room is closer to the lobby, and before long he finds himself at his door. He fumbles with the key card, swearing under his breath. Finally, the light turns green, and he steps through the door. He sets the milkshake on the nightstand and heads into the bathroom. He turns the shower on, strips out of his clothes, and steps under the water. Wolf closes his eyes as the water eases the tension out of his back and shoulders.

In her room, Cal is sitting on the chez lounge while alternating between drinking her milkshake, writing in her journal, and texting with William. It's times like this she misses having her friend nearby. Of course, they would be driven to the camp by truck according to the paperwork, so there is no reason William can't join them. Cal has asked, practically begging for him to join them. He keeps telling her he can't as he has other plans. Finally, she gives up, and the two resort to idle chit-chat about their lives.

Cal says goodnight to William, shuts her journal, and sets it on the nightstand. The empty milkshake cup is tossed in the trash. Cal makes sure her door is locked, then steps into the bathroom to take a hot shower. The water is turned on, Cal strips naked, then steps under the spray of scalding water. She sits on the floor, hugging her knees to her chest, and rests her forehead on them. Drown out by the sound of the running water, Cal sobs big body wracking sobs. The entire day finally collapses on her, and she cries with abandon. Taking a few deep breaths, she pulls herself to her feet and washes slowly. Each motion from grabbing her shampoo to rinsing her hair was slow, deliberate. Once out of the shower, she dries off and takes a moment to look at herself in the mirror. The lights are shut off as she leaves the bathroom, and crosses to her bed. She sets the alarm on her phone, climbs into bed, and collapses under the blankets. Cal is asleep almost before her head hits the pillow.

It's a fitful sleep, filled with nightmares and memories. She dreams of their cabin in Wyoming, and the jade dragon statue that some say cursed her and Wolf. Cal dreams of her hospital stay and the cave collapse in China. She dreams of Zion and Oxide. These dreams cause her to toss and turn for several hours before they subside, and she is finally able to sleep peacefully.

November 15th

I made it to LA. Was too tired to write yesterday. I met Mr. Maximov. It was an easy meeting aside from Wolf being there. He is my bodyguard for this dig. It seems Mr. Maximov's boss hired him, since we have worked together in the past. We'll get through it.

I can't believe he is here. I can't believe they hired that asshole. He is still handsome, the same rugged good looks I imagine Rhory would have inherited. Dark hair and dark eyes. I can only imagine how much my son would have looked like him.

And don't get me started on that damn smile. Why am I still gushing over him like a high school girl? Because I still love him. At least I know they hired the best to keep me safe out there.

November 15th later in the day.

We had a chance to talk. Well, as much as we talk. He wanted to make sure I was healing. We were mean to each other. I can't believe he still wears his wedding band, but the tan line doesn't lie. I still wear mine, but at least I moved them to my right hand. No, he wears his on his left as if he is still married. Maybe he did remarry or is planning on it. None of my business.

After our talk, we went to dinner. The route took us by an Elephant Bar. I haven't been by one since the shooting. Not sure what happened. I was fine, then Wolf was holding me, and my heart was beating against my ribs like I had just run a marathon. I was crying and I couldn't breathe. Next thing I know, I shoved him off me and jumped out of the truck. I don't care how comfortable and safe I felt at that moment, he doesn't get to do that anymore. He needs to learn to keep his hands to himself.

But, oh, this cologne, the one that smells like sandalwood, cedar, and bourbon. The smell of gunpowder clings to his skin as if he just stepped off the gun range. He is still so caring, even took the long way back to the hotel, so I didn't have to see the restaurant again. I wanted to invite him back to my room to spend time together, but we are going to be trapped at a campsite and, well, I don't want to say the wrong thing and screw up.

I always say the wrong thing and screw things up. I really should be getting some sleep. I have an early flight tomorrow. While I love Egypt, I want this dig to be over with already.

- Cal

Chapter 4

Early the next morning, Cal's alarm pulls her from a sound sleep. She blindly swings at the phone, sending it off the table and across the low pile carpet. Sitting up, eyes still half-closed, Cal swears under her breath. She swings her legs off the bed and stands. A few slow, stiff steps, and she leans down to pick up her phone. Cal straightens up, grimacing at a twinge in her back near where the bullet had made its exit. She makes her way toward the bathroom, wincing at the sight of herself in the mirror.

Her hair stands up in all directions and her skin is overly pale and sickly looking. Cal turns on the shower and sticks her head under the spray. She wets her hair down before turning the water off. Grabbing a towel, she scrubs her hair dry. Cal makes her way back to the main room, digging her hairbrush out of her bag. As she pulls the brush through the knotted mess that is her hair, Cal tries to plan out how to pack her bags. She looks at her open duffle bag, eyes falling on the mismatched set of pistols and the boxes of ammo. This complicates things. The guns and ammo can't be together in the belly of the plane, and neither can go in her carry-on. *I may have to check both bags,* she thinks as she drops the brush onto the bed.

Cal rummages through her duffle bag to find an outfit for the day. For the first time in months, Cal looks at clothes. She thinks about the colors that Wolf prefers on her, and how her clothes fit. Why is she worried about looking nice for someone she divorced? She rests her hand on the edge of the bag, taking a deep breath. Cal reminds herself she only has to look nice for herself. Finally, she settles on a pair of black denim shorts and a blue-grey tank top. She looks down at her scar-covered left knee and shrugs. Cal had learned long ago to be proud of her scars. She returns to the bathroom, packs up her toiletries, takes another moment to glance at herself in the mirror, smiling brightly, before returning to the main room to finish packing.

At the other side of the hotel. Wolf is also packing and having the ammo dilemma. He is dressed in blue jeans, and a black t-shirt, after also debating with himself about what to wear. Once he is satisfied that everything has been packed, he leaves the room and makes his way to the front desk.

Cal stands there, checking out when Wolf approaches. He stands behind her, smiling softly to himself. She thanks the clerk and turns, jumping when she finds herself almost face to face with Wolf. Cal steps aside. The smile on his face never faltering as Wolf steps up so he can also check out. By the door, Cal waits as she would have in the good days of their relationship. When he is done, Wolf joins her at the door.

"How're you taking your guns?" she asks as they step out of the hotel and into the warm sunlight of southern California. Cal looks at him, tilting her head slightly. Wolf shrugs.

"I was going to ask you the same thing," Wolf replies honestly. Cal nibbles nervously at her lower lip as they approach her Jeep. She pulls the key from her pocket, unlocking the truck. She tugs the door up, setting her duffle bag in the back with her old canvas bag lying next to it. Wolf can't help but chuckle at the sight of that battered or climbing bag.

"I mean, if you want, we can put the ammo in one bag and the guns in another," Cal says, doing her best to sound nonchalant. Wolf blinks, watching her. He leans against the side of her vehicle. The silence makes Cal uncomfortable. She reaches out, adjusting her bags not that they needed any adjusting.

"Yeah, we might as well. Here or at the airport?" Wolf finally says, standing upright.

"Here. It might look weird if we're playing with firearms at the airport," she smirks as she unzips her bag. She flips the bag open, carefully lifting out the boxes of ammo.

"You know you love those strip searches," Wolf chuckles.

"Only when..." she starts then abruptly stops. Her cheeks tinged pink as she hands him the ammo boxes.

"Only when?" He asks with a knowing smirk. Wolf trades the ammunition for the pistols.

"Never mind," she snaps as she takes the firearms from him. Cal focuses on what she is doing, trying to hide her deepening blush. They are gently nestled among her clothes so that nothing smashes together in transit. Wolf walks off to his truck, still chucking to himself. Cal slams her trunk shut, cussing under her breath as she gets in the driver's seat. She doesn't check her review mirror for Wolf and doesn't wait for him, instead, she zips out into traffic and heads for the airport.

Cal hates LA traffic and the airport. She has always hated them. Cal lived not too far from Los Angeles before her dad's career drug them to New Mexico. The only fond memory she has of the city was the one time her team got to play softball on the Dodgers practice field. Her grandparents are still just over the mountains, and she has plans to visit them on her return trip. She checks traffic in her rearview mirror, not at all surprised to see his truck behind her. After all, they are traveling in the same direction to the same location.

Wolf follows behind her, humming along to the radio. *We could have ridden together;* he thinks as he guides the truck through morning traffic. He can't wait to get out of Los Angeles, hell, out of the states. After months of doing simple security, this will be a nice change of pace. Wolf, like Cal, enjoys traveling. He loves seeing new places, meeting interesting people even if he does have to shoot them on occasion. Shooting people is the least fun part of his job with all the paperwork it causes. If he has his way, this trip will be problem-free. Of course, Cal is the lead on this trip, so he knows that trouble is bound to happen.

Cal and Wolf both pull off the freeway, following their exit toward the twisting maze of roads that is LAX. Cal finds long-term parking not too far from the door. She climbs out of her vehicle, watching Wolf drive by. She leaves the driver's door open as she walks to the back of the Jeep and opens the trunk. The duffle bag is sat on the ground next to her vehicle, while she settles her backpack onto her shoulders. The trunk is shut then she walks to the door and hits the lock button before shutting in. She grabs the handle of her duffle bag, walking toward to main door and the ticket desk.

She plans to try to get checked in and through security before Wolf can join her. Cal strides through the airport with a sense of purpose. She weaves through the crowds of travelers, making a beeline for the ticket booth. As soon as the first agent is available, Cal walks over and sets her bag on the scale before setting her backpack at her feet. From the top pouch, she pulls her ID, passport, and confirmation which are all handed to the lady. She waits as patiently as possible as the woman types in all the information and get Cal checked into her flight. As always, the pistols being declared causes a few minutes of delay but everything else goes smoothly. With her bag checked Cal slings her climbing back over her shoulder and walks off toward security with her paperwork in hand.

So far so good on her plan to beat Wolf to the gate and get a seat safe from his ever-watchful eyes. The security line is long but is moving quickly. Cal shuffles forward, kicking her shoes off. She leans down and picks them up on the floor. Her cellphone is pulled from her bag. The bag goes on the belt. Her shoes and the cellphone go into a bin, and she runs her hands over her pockets to make sure she didn't forget anything. Finding her Jeep key, she tucks that into the top pouch on her backpack.

She walks through the metal detector. There is no chirp and Cal will take that as a good sign. She walks over to the end of the conveyor belt, grabbing her boots and cellphone, which she tucks in her back pocket. She drops her boots to the floor, stuffing her feet into them while her bag gets a thorough searching. Once the bag is handed over, Cal makes sure all the pockets are zipped and slings it onto one shoulder. She steps out of security, pausing only long enough to tie her boots.

Now for the trek to the gate, she thinks. Her gate is never near security. After all, she isn't that lucky. Behind her, there is a whistle. She tries to ignore and keep walking. It could be anyone whistling for anyone else. They're in a busy crowded airport after all. As she hears fast footsteps approaching her, she slides her arm through the other shoulder strap, so she doesn't lose her backpack. A large hand grabs her shoulder, and she turns. Her left fist comes up, aiming for whoever has grabbed her. The figure's other hand closes on her wrist, preventing her from punching him in the face.

"Cal! Chill! It's me!" Wolf says, still holding her by the wrist. She blinks at him. They stand like that for a few seconds while Cal's brain catches up with everything going on. A few TSA agents and security guards watch the two just in case they need to step in to break something up. She yanks her arm away, turns back around, and resumes her walk towards the gate.

"You should know better." She snaps as Wolf falls into step beside her.

"Sorry thought you heard me whistle for you," Wolf replies. Cal rubs her wrist where he grabbed it. The joint doesn't hurt, but she can still feel the warmth of his skin and the callouses on his hands. The feeling leaves her conflicted, both repulsed and comforted.

"I'm not some dog to come when you whistle Wolf," she smirks as she speaks.

"But you can be a bitch," Wolf retorts. Once again, the words are out before he can stop them, except this time he doesn't regret them. He doesn't need to spare her feelings.

"I always thought you liked that about me," she replies. Her eyes stay focused on the gate number ahead. Wolf laughs quietly. For that moment, it feels like old times. The two of them roasting each other as they walked through the airport. They both know the feeling won't last and for now, they enjoy it. Cal stops briefly at a small shop for a bottle of water and chocolate. She takes this time to tuck her paperwork back into her bag. Wolf waits for her before the two continue their walk.

They find seats against the wall, watching the crowd. Cal sips her water and nibbles on her chocolate bar. Tears burn the back of her eyes as memories fill her head and threaten to spill down her cheeks. She remembers them sitting in the terminal, waiting to fly to Ireland. It was her last big trip after finding out she was pregnant. It was the flight when Wolf confronted her over the Atlantic about the appointment card he had found. He had proposed on the spot, with the diamond ring she currently has nestled safely in her duffle bag.

She scrubs her hand across her eyes and focuses on the crowd around them. Every few minutes she feels Wolf's eyes on her. She continues to snack, flipping through emails on her phone, and fights the urge to look at him. No more information about who they're meeting or who is on the team.

She finishes the chocolate bar, leaving the wrapper resting on her leg. Wolf reaches over, carefully picking up the wrapper so as not to touch her thigh. He takes it over to the garbage can and returns to his seat. Cal looks at him, then returns to watching the crowd.

"They should be starting to board any minute now," Wolf says as two flight attendants approach the gate. Cal follows his gaze and nods. She leans forward, digging her passport and ticket out. The bag is rezipped, and the water bottle is safely tucked into one of the side pouches before she leans back in her seat. Wolf taps his foot impatiently, waiting for the rows to start being called. Wolf pulls out his ticket and passport. Cal shifts in her seat, feeling a bit anxious. She just wants this part to be over and to be on the job site already. The flight attendants start calling rows toward the back of the plane. Cal stands, lifting her backpack. She settles the bag onto her back and adjusts it to be more comfortable. One hand holds her phone, ticket, and passport, while the fingers of the other hand tap on her leg as she takes her place in line. Wolf follows her, making sure to stand next to her.

"What're we going to do for nine hours in France?" Wolf asks. Cal looks at him, blinking as if she had forgotten they were traveling together. She shrugs in response and turns back to face the gate. As their row is called, they start the slow shuffle toward the ticket desk then toward the plane.

"I'm stuck in France with you for nine hours. Ugh." Cal says, one side of her lip pulling up in a disgusted sneer. She keeps her attention ahead of her, not looking at him. She hadn't looked at how long the layovers were.

"Ya know. There's a lot that can be done in those nine hours," Wolf grins. Cal glares over her shoulder at him. "Never mind. Forget I said anything," he mutters. The attendants motion them to their seats, and they start the shuffle down the narrow path between seats. Behind her, before she is out of earshot, Cal hears Wolf talking to someone which is followed by a flirty giggle that is drowned out by the sound of the passengers.

She slides into her seat, setting her bag between her feet. Cal opens the top pouch and slides her passport and tickets back into the bag before tucking it under the seat in front of her. She leans back in her seat, buckling her seatbelt. She is a bit sad to see they are over the wing.

"Well, well imagine meeting you here," Wolf's voice pulls eyes from the window to his face. She sighs, rolls her eyes, and looks back out the window. He slides his own back under the seat in front of him and settles back in a bid to get comfortable. Cal crosses her arms over her stomach. Wolf lays a white scrap of paper on his leg as he buckles his seatbelt. He makes sure she can read the curly handwriting that spells out Mardi and a number. The I, of course, dotted with a heart which doesn't surprise Cal. She glances at it; eyes narrowing at the sight but she tries not to let it bother her.

Hastily, and feigning embarrassment, Wolf slides the paper into his pocket. He didn't get the outward reaction from her he wanted but it was enough of one. The safety video plays, Cal ignores it and her seatmate. She wants off this plane, to quit this job, and go back to Albuquerque. She wants away from Wolf most of all. A job at the museum had been offered to her and at this moment, she is considering taking it.

The flight attendants start making their last rounds before take-off. Wolf is chatting with a petite blond woman with a faint French accent. Cal can only imagine this is Mardi who dots her Is with little hearts. The blond giggles at something Wolf has said. Cal isn't paying attention to the conversation but assumes it's unfunny. Mardi pats Wolf on the shoulder before she straightens up and makes her way back toward her seat. Leaning back in his seat, a self-satisfied smirk played across his features. Seeing this, Cal rolls his eyes.

"Jealous?" Wolf asks, his voice low.

"Nah, I always got taught to share my old toys with those less fortunate," Cal says, staring at the window. Wolf grumbles under his breath, shifting slightly in his seat. She smiles to herself, watching what she can see of the tarmac. The plane starts down the runway, jostling as it picks up speed. The wheels come off the ground and Cal closes her hand on the armrest, gripping it until her knuckles are white. Wolf watches her before turning his attention to the inflight magazine. Usually, he would play on his phone, or answer emails but his attention span just isn't' here for that at the moment. So, he just aimlessly flips through the pages of all the useless things money can buy. Cal keeps her attention out the window until they are at cruising altitude.

Only then does she relax enough to pull her journal and pen from her bag. Cal sets the book and pen in her lap, zipping the bag back up and pushing it under the seat. She opens the book to a blank page, smoothing it down as she clicks the pen. She writes the dates, and what little she knows about the dig. It's not a very long entry but she is sure the others will be. Feeling eyes burning into the side of her head, she slowly closes the book then latches it. The pen is laid on the front cover and she folds her hands over it. She doesn't look at Wolf, instead, Cal looks around the cabin.

"This is going to be a long flight," Wolf mutters to no one in particular.

"Go chat with your friend Mardi," Cal replies. The words came out sharper than she meant for them, too.

"I would, but she's working," Wolf replies as the little blond saunters her way up the aisle toward a call bell. He leans over a bit, getting a better view as Mardi leans down to talk to the passenger. Cal rolls her eyes, shifting in her seat so her back is turned slightly to him. She pulls her journal closer to her, fingers digging into the leather cover. Cal knows that his flirting shouldn't bother her. She divorced him after all, but to see him show interest in another woman twists her guts and makes her heart ache.

Wolf knows it bothers her, but that is what he wants. If she is paying attention, she would see how half-assed his flirting is. It's all done just to get a rise out of Cal, to prove to himself she still loves him enough to get mad or jealous. Cal slides her journal back into her bag, just as Mardi comes around to take drink orders.

"Drinks for either of you?" The blond asks. Cal swears her accent gets thicker as she leans down closer to Wolf.

"Coffee" Cal keeps her answer short and simple.

"Me too," Wolf says.

"Cream or sugar?" She asks Wolf, not even acknowledging Cal.

"No, thank you, hun," Wolf replies, handing the first cup of coffee to Cal. She lowers her tray and sets the mug down. Her hands stay wrapped around the Styrofoam cup. Wolf takes the second cup she offers. Mardi offers a small wave, just a wiggle of the fingertips, then moves onto the next passenger. Cal sips her coffee, looking out the window. The liquid is hot and the burning sensation is weirdly comforting.

I can't handle this. I can barely be on a flight with him, how am I going to deal with him for days on end? Cal thinks, sipping her coffee.

I shouldn't have agreed to this. Wolf thinks, chugging his still hot coffee. He winces, inhaling sharply, as the scalding liquid burns its way down his throat.

"Should've let it cool off first, you dumbass," Cal says, glancing at Wolf. He glares at her, shaking his head ever so slightly. She laughs, folding her tray up before sipping her coffee again. Wolf finds his glare softens to something almost like a smile as he watches her. Just like in the past, he is taken in by the depths of those soft blue-green eyes. Guilt grips his chest as he watches her. Cal turns, catching him staring.

"Can I help you?" she asks, sharply. Wolf just shakes his head and turns his attention to the other passengers on the plane. "Whatever," she says, gulping down the rest of her coffee. She reaches over and drops her empty cup into his, just as she had any other time they traveled together. Cal settles back into the seat, closing her eyes and listening to the cabin. She dozes off into a light sleep. Wolf isn't far behind her.

The rest of the flight is uneventful. The plane starts its descent, waking up the two explorers. Cal shifts and fidgets as the plane continues downward. Landing announcements play over the speakers in both French and English. Cal takes a deep breath as the tires bounce and squeal over the tarmac. The plane taxis to the gate and the travelers start gathering their things. Almost in unison, Wolf and Cal unbuckle, pull their bag out from under the seats and set them on their laps until the plane stops fully.

They both stand, bags going over one shoulder. It's almost a slower shuffle deplaning than boarding. Cal mutters to herself as they move forward. Wolf keeps a close eye on her and the surrounding crowd. Now he is in full work mode. Cal barely notices the change in his demeanor, her focus is on getting off the plane. Mardi lights up when she sees Wolf coming her way.

"Someone is excited to see you," Cal says in a snarky sing-song voice under her breath. She smirks, stepping from the plane to the jet bridge. Before the echo of the hallway drowns out Wolf, Cal hears a whispered conversation and a loud slap. Wolf emerges from the crowd rubbing the red handprint forming on his jaw. "Offend her delicate sensibilities?" Cal asks, only semi-curious.

"Just had to tell her I wouldn't be calling. I have my eye on someone else," Wolf admits. Cal's heart crumbles. She hopes she has done well enough to keep the reaction off her face and eyes.

He's moved on. You should too, she tells herself. Cal keeps that half-smile plastered on her face, although it no longer reaches her eyes. She turns and leads the way to their next gate. Wolf follows her, unsure of how to take her reaction. The smile never faltered, but he had seen the amusement in her eyes melt to sadness. Wolf walks faster, closing the gap between them until he is walking alongside her. Cal tenses as he walks so close to her, their arms almost brush against each other.

November 16th

We are on the plane to France. Wolf got a phone number from some stewardess named Mardi. What kind of adult dots their I with a heart? Her, that's who.

Ok, back to work. We are heading to Egypt, looking for an ankh pendant with the Eye of Horus in the center. That is all we know. We have learned nothing else about this dig. We don't even know who is picking us up at the airport. The only other thing we have been told is the organizer and buyer have supplied all the tents, raised cots, and blankets. More when I know more.

-Cal

Chapter 5

It's a short but crowded hike from one gate to the next. The international terminal is closed off from the rest of the airport, but still contains shops and a few small eateries. Cal finds herself a seat against one wall, where she can see most of the waiting area. She slides her bag off, sitting it between her feet as she sits down. Wolf removes his bag, sliding it under his chair before sitting next to Cal. He keeps an eye on anyone who came near the two of them, mentally noting builds and distinguishing features.

Cal watches people too, but she is not noting their looks. She watches how close they got to her. Cal looks down at her hands, making sure they are not reaching for anything. Her body is tense, and her eyes dart over the crowd. In her chest, her heart beats against her ribs. She tries to relax, but can't. She can't even fake it. Wolf reaches over, resting his hand on her forearm. Cal pulls away, narrowing her eyes at him.

"I'm fine," she snaps before he can even ask. Wolf pulls his hand away and shrugs. In reality, she just wants to fall into his arms and let his warm embrace ease her anxiety.

"If you say so," Wolf replies. He stands, stretching. "I'm going to grab dinner. What do you want?"

"Surprise me," Cal shrugs. Wolf nods then walks off. Her gaze follows him as he weaves his way through the crowd. Even after she loses him in the crowd, she watches. Whichever girl Wolf has his eye on is lucky, Cal thinks sadly. She pulls her eyes away from the direction Wolf disappeared and resumes scanning the crowd. There are travelers of all types, many of them seem split between business travelers and tourists. Cal and Wolf could pass for a couple of tourists, even with the climbing bags. The crowd parts and Wolf comes walking through it.

She smiles at the sight of him carrying sandwiches and soda. Her stomach growls and grumbles as he gets closer. Wolf hands her a turkey and swiss sub, then returns to his seat. He passes her a soda, setting his drink on the floor between his feet. Cal follows suit, then pulls the wrapper off her sandwich. Taking a large bite, she sighs happily as she chews. Wolf chuckles, then opens his.

"Thanks. This is delicious." Cal says after swallowing her food. The fact that he remembered her favorite sandwich and ordered it brings her some comfort. She eats a few more bites before leaning down and picking up her soda. With the sandwich balanced on her lap, she opens the soda and takes a long drink. Wolf has his sandwich half gone. They don't talk while they eat. Cal isn't sure what she'd say anyway. She crumples the wrapper as she chews the last bite of her sub. She sets her soda back down, holding her hand out for the trash. Wolf has a few bites of his meal left, but hands over the paper wrapping. Cal squishes it into a ball and makes the short walk to the trash can. Wolf keeps a watchful eye on her as she throws out the trash and makes her way back to their seats.

Cal sits back down, leaning in her seat and watching the crowd. Wolf finishes his meal, wiping his crumbs from his face. He also watches the people around them. Cal pulls her cell phone from her pocket, checking for new emails. There is nothing. No emails or texts. Now she is beginning to worry.

"Still no team update?" Wolf says, looking over her shoulder. She locks her phone.

"Nope. Not a damn thing. It's starting to make me a bit nervous." Cal sighs, tucking the phone back into her pocket. "I don't even know who is picking us up at the airport.

"I'm sure it'll be fine," Wolf tries to sound reassuring. She smiles softly at him, offering a lazy shrug.

"It's gonna have to be fine," Cal looks at Wolf, then adds, "Or it'll just be me coming out of the desert."

"You wouldn't shoot me," Wolf rolls his eyes.

"You know I would though," Cal says, completely serious. She offers him a tense smile, then turns her attention back to the terminal. "Who the hell decided to do long layovers for international flights." She adds, changing the topic.

"Go for a walk if you want. I'll watch the bags." Wolf says. Cal stands, lifting her bag onto her shoulders.

"I know better than to leave my stuff with you." She adjusts the bag, then wanders off toward the shops. Wolf laughs, watching her go. The laughter and smile fade into a frown as he remembers the night he had read her journal. The night he found out that she loved him. He let out a weary sigh, sad that those days are gone.

Wolf watches the crowd, keeping an eye open for Cal's return. He tells himself he should have gone with her. He is supposed to be her bodyguard, after all. Wolf fidgets in his seat, checking the time. Cal hasn't been gone that long, but he is ready to go looking for her. Unable to wait any longer. Wolf scoops his bag up and stands in one motion. The bag is settled on his shoulders, he grabs the sodas off the floor, then strides off through the crowd. He walks slowly along the row of shops, glancing at each one. There are only a few he can imagine Cal in. As he finds these shops, he walks through them slowly. After clearing a bookstore, and an outdoor store, he continues down the line. Ahead of him, Cal is walking through a shop full of sweets. Generally, she tries to watch what she eats, but sugary treats are always good before a long trip. Cal pauses at one of the shelves, looking over the jars and their labels. Wolf spots her from the door and makes his way toward her.

Cal is holding a small glass jar with a paintbrush tied to it. The label reads Chocolate Body Paint in red letters on a cream-colored label. There are instructions for warming and use. Wolf reads over her shoulder, "got someone in mind?" He asks. His voice borders on a growl. She jumps, almost dropping the container. Carefully, she sets the bottle back on the shelf. The warmth of his breath on her neck and ear sends a chill down her spine.

"Wouldn't you like to know?" she asks with a sly smile before walking away. Cal grabs a couple of small bags of chocolates and takes them to the register. She pays for her candies, then tucks them into her bag before she walks out of the store and heads back toward their seats. Wolf watches her, then grabs the glass container. He takes it to the register and pays for it. The cashier, who saw the exchange between the two, offers Wolf a knowing smile as the transaction finishes. Wolf steps out into the hallway, sets his bag at his feet. He takes a moment to stash the jar among his change of clothes before he zips the bag. Wolf returns the bag to his shoulders and walks toward their seats.

He scans the people, spotting Cal. The crowd has thinned out as flights have left, making it easier to find each other. Wolf makes his way across the terminal and toward where she shifts. Cal is typing away on her phone, a slight smirk playing across her face. Wolf watches her for a few seconds before setting his bag down and sitting next to her.

"Texting the boyfriend?" Wolf asks, his voice faltering some.

"Nope. William. He's on his way to see Bernd," she replies. "Was that a note of jealousy I just heard?"

"Nah, just wanted to know who I should be sending a condolence card to." Wolf tries to cover his momentary mistake.

"Funny," Cal says flatly, focusing her attention on her phone. It buzzes in her hand, she opens the message and taps out a quick response. Cal slides the phone into her back pocket. Wolf watches her out of the corner of her eye. The two people watch and listen to the crowds. They take turns glancing at each other when the other isn't looking. Throughout their wait, the two take turns getting up and walking around. With each passing hour, Cal develops a slight limp. Her scarred left knee tends to get stiff after sitting for too long.

Flight attendants approach the front desk directly in front of the gate. Wolf and Cal both sit up. The attendants start shuffling papers and typing on their keyboards. Cal taps her foot, impatiently waiting. Wolf rests his hand on her knee, trying to calm her. She smacks his hand, glaring. The attendants start announcing the rows.

"I told you to keep your hands to yourself. I will stab you," she says with a sickly-sweet smile.

"Your knife is in your other bag," Wolf points out.

"I don't need a knife. I have a pen." She replies, that smile never faltering. As the other passengers start lining up for their respective seats, Cal stands. She lifts her bag, setting it on one shoulder. She makes her way over to the lines. Wolf grabs his bag by its handle and follows her. They stand together in silence, patiently waiting. Cal sets her bag down, digging her ticket and passport from the bag before it's rezipped and returned to her back. Wolf does the same, retrieving his ticket before setting his bag on his back. As soon as all the preferred and first-class passengers are loaded, the rows for the back of the plane start filing aboard. This flight will take them to Cairo where they will stay the night before getting picked up and driven to the job the next day. Cal is hoping for separate rooms. She feels like that will not happen with the way the rest of the job goes.

Wolf does his best to keep a safe distance from her while trying to still be close enough to her just in case he is needed. Cal crosses her arms over her stomach, trying to put more space between them. Wolf keeps an eye on her as they walk. He has been hired as her bodyguard and that is just what he is going to do even if she doesn't want him to. Cal makes her way into the crowd, intentionally putting people between her and Wolf. He cusses under her breath, trying to weave through the crowd to catch up with her. He tries as hard as he can, but he can't get people to move, and can't catch up to her.

Cal makes her way onto the plane and toward her seat. She enjoys the few free minutes away from Wolf and those sharp eyes. Those eyes she keeps finding herself getting lost in. Cal is happy to see that her seat is on the exit row. She returns her ticket and passport to her bag before she puts them in the overhead storage. She slides into the seat and buckles her seatbelt. Wolf comes down the aisle, looking unimpressed with her. Not that she cares. Cal shifts in her seat, focusing her attention out the window.

Wolf puts his ticket and passport away. He slides his bag next to hers in the overhead compartment, then drops into the seat next to her with a grunt. Cal doesn't bother to look at him. Wolf watches the other passengers as he buckles his seatbelt. The last of the passengers board and find their seats. The two of them sit in silence that can almost pass for comfortable. The plane moves and begins to taxi toward the runway. Cal fidgets in her seat. She watches the lights on the runway.

At the front of the plane, the flight attendants are going through the safety information. All the instructions are done in both French and English. Cal and Wolf pay very little attention to this. When the speech is done, the flight attendants take their seats. Cal's hand fumbles for the armrest as the plane accelerates. Her hand finds Wolf's forearm instead, her nails digging into his flesh. Wolf inhales sharply, causing Cal to turn quickly. She looks down, pulling her hand away and leaving little crescent moon shapes in his arm.

"Sorry," Cal says, only about half meaning it.

"No, you're not," Wolf smirks. "You never worried about clawing me in the past," he offers that predatory smile, which makes her blush faintly. Cal looks out the window, realizing they are airborne. It'll be late when they reach Cairo, and Cal is determined to stay awake. Wolf watches the other passengers, running his left hand over the nail marks in his right arm. They sting, but he doesn't mind. Cal glances at them again, then back out the window.

As always happens when they travel, Cal and Wolf doze in and out of sleep. The plane jostling across the tarmac wakes them both up. Cal grabs for the arm of the chair again. Her hand closes around his wrist, she squeezes it without digging her nails in. They both look out the window as the plane pulls up to the jet way. Cal taps her foot, and Wolf fidgets. They are eager to get off this plane and on their way to the hotel. They are desperate for a hot shower, comfortable beds, and tomorrow they want to meet the rest of their team. The plane stops and everyone stands in almost perfect unison. Cal and Wolf are no different as they step out into the aisle to get their bags. Wolf grabs both of them, handing Cal hers. They settle their bags onto their backs. This time, Wolf grabs one of the loops on her bag so as not to lose her.

Cal leads the way off the plane, and up the ramp toward the airport. Wolf follows her as they weave their way through the crowds toward the baggage claim. Standing at the carousel is a man in a very sharp-looking suit. In his hands, he holds a sign that reads "Dr. and Mr. Corrigan" in bold letters. They both see it and feel instant sadness. The carousel comes to life, dropping bags onto the conveyor belt. Wolf grabs both their bags and hands Cal hers. They approach the man, who holds one hand out to Wolf.

"Dr. Corrigan, nice to meet you," the man says. He hadn't read his sign.

"I'm Dr. Coburn, no longer Corrigan," Cal says. "That's Mr. Corrigan." She points to Wolf. If this is how this is starting, she can only imagine how it will look in the field.

"My apologies." He says, then motions for them to follow. They walk behind him, dodging between people before stepping out into the hot desert air. The man opens the back door to a long black limo. Cal hands her bags to Wolf, who helps the man put them in the trunk. She slides into the large luxury car. Wolf follows her. The door shuts and the man climbs into the driver's seat. The car is guided through the busy Cairo traffic with ease. The driver pulls up to the Paradise Boutique Hotel. The man parks the car and hops out of the vehicle. He opens the door for them, then removes their bags from the trunk. Cal and Wolf shoulder their bags and grab their duffle bags before heading into the hotel. She goes to the front desk to check in. There is a moment of absolute confusion as the desk clerk hands her two keys.

"The reservation is for two in one of our one-bedroom suites," the clerk says. Cal turns, handing Wolf his key. She doesn't wait for him and walks off toward the elevator. Wolf jogs after her. They step into the elevator and make their way up to their room. Cal mutters as she swipes the key card and lets them into the room. She doesn't leave any space for a debate, striding toward the bedroom.

"Where am I —" Wolf starts.

"Sleep on the couch for all I care," Cal interrupts as she shuts the bedroom door. Cal tosses her bags against one wall and strips out of her travel clothes. She pulls out a pair of cotton PJ pants and a tank top. Cal dresses quickly and verifies the bedroom door is latched. She climbs into bed, skips writing, and lays there staring at the ceiling. Cal listens to Wolf's movements in the living room. It's not long before Cal falls into a deep, dreamless sleep.

In the living room, Wolf changes into his pajamas. He grabs extra pillows and a blanket from the closet before making himself as comfortable as he can on the hotel's couch. Wolf listens to the sounds of the hotel, listening for her until he finally dozes off. His sleep is fitful.

Chapter 6

Early the next morning, Cal is awoken by a quiet knock on the door. She sits up, blinking in the bright light that peeks through the curtains. Climbing from the bed, she rubs her eyes and makes her way across to the door. Putting on her best glare, Cal tugs the door open. Wolf offers a small guilty smile.

"Sorry. Didn't mean to wake you up." Wolf says quietly. He takes in the sight of her standing there. Cal's hair is a mess. The cotton PJ pants hang low on her hips, and the tank top has ridden up just enough to show her stomach. It also shows the scars and one small tattoo. Wolf doesn't remember seeing the tattoo before. Seeing the scar, he feels a pang of sadness and guilt.

"You're not sorry." She snaps. "What the fuck do you want, Wolf?" Cal narrows her eyes at him.

"It's just about time for us to get packed up and head out," Wolf says, pulling his eyes from her stomach to a spot just over her shoulder. He can't look directly at her without his eyes traveling to those scars.

"Fine." She replies, slamming the door in his face. Wolf stands there for a minute or two before he turns back to his room. Cal rubs her eyes again as she makes her way to the bathroom. She turns the shower on, stripping out of her pajamas as the water warms up. Cal steps into the spray, letting the hot water run over her body and carrying her worries down the drain.

Meanwhile, Wolf is double-checking that everything is packed. His toiletry bag is tucked into his duffle bag, and he makes sure both of his bags are zipped and ready to go. Wolf has left out just a single change of clothes. He hears the shower shut off, staring at the door to the bedroom. In there , she steps out of the bathroom and walks toward her bag. She pulls on a pair of jeans, and a tank top, then repacks her bag. She opens the bedroom door. Cal stuffs her feet into her boots and ties them.

"Bathroom is free," she calls to him. He slips past her with his clothes tucked under one arm and disappears into the bathroom. The door shuts and the shower turns on.

Cal tucks her clean-up kit into her larger bag and takes one last look around the room. Satisfied that everything is packed, Cal grabs her key and lifts both her bags. Wolf finishes up his shower, coming out of the bathroom dressed in jeans, and his hiking boots. He doesn't say anything as he grabs his key, bags, and heads for the lobby without a word. Cal does another double-check of the room before she leaves. Cal meets Wolf in the lobby, taking his key. She heads to the desk, checking out. When she turns around, Wolf is already walking out the door to meet the large Jeep that is parked out front.

Cal follows him, seeing a familiar figure sitting behind the wheel. As Cal and Wolf move to the trunk, the driver climbs out of the vehicle.

Standing over six feet tall, Brock looks like a life-size GI Joe. Salt and pepper hair is worn high and tight. His blue eyes are sharp and icy. Crows' feet appear at the corners of his eyes as he smiles. He watches as Cal's brain catches up as he walks around the back of the truck. Cal slides her backpack off, letting it hit the ground.

"Brock!!" She yells, running over to him. Cal throws her arms around him in a big hug. He lifts her off the ground, spinning her around before gently setting her back on her feet. "What're you doing here? I thought you were retired!"

"I am, but I like to pick up an easy job," Brock says, motioning the Jeep.

"But I don't need two bodyguards." She motions to Wolf. Her lip curls up slightly at the thought of Wolf being her bodyguard. "Let's leave him behind. You and I like old times. Whatcha say?" Cal grins.

"Wolf is still your only bodyguard. I'm just your driver." Brock motions for their bags. "It's my job to get you there and back safely. Both of you."

Cal nods, walking back over to her bags. She shoulders the backpack and pulls her duffle bag closer to the trunk. She loads the duffle bag, then lays her backpack on top of it. Once her bags are loaded, Cal walks toward the passenger door. Wolf loads his bags next to hers, then pulls the trunk shut. He sees Cal has already settled in the passenger seat, so he slides into the back seat, behind Brock. Their driver and friend, is already behind the wheel, tapping his hands.

"Ready?" Brock asks, looking from the mirror to Cal and back again. The two adventurers nod. Brock starts the truck, pulling out of the parking lot, and onto the road. Cal looks out the window, tapping her fingers on her legs. "Excited to be back to work?" Brock asks, glancing at his friend.

"Yeah. It's gonna be nice to be back in the field. I wonder who else got hired," Cal glances over her shoulder at Wolf, momentarily locking eyes with him. She turns her attention back out the window. "It's awesome to have you back, Brock."

"Don't get used to it," the man chuckles. "I was bored, and you know how I love Egypt." Cal laughs quietly.

"We'll make sure this is a good trip, then," Wolf speaks up from the backseat. Cal nods.

"I'm just the driver. I get to drop you off at camp, then drive back to Cairo, where I will be staying in a five-star hotel and playing tourist while you two are roughing it in the desert.

I will be back in four or five days to pick you both up," Brock smiles as he talks.

"You're getting soft in your old days, Brock," Cal laughs, giving him a playful slug in the arm.

"What can I say? I've gotten used to comfortable beds and room service," Brock laughs as he guides the SUV out of the city and onto the back roads. "How've you been, Cal?"

She shrugs, "getting better." A soft smile spreads across her face as she watches the city give way to desert sands. Wolf watches her, and seeing her smile makes him smile.

"That's good to hear. I've been worried about you. You keep falling out of touch," Brock tries not to lecture, but he can't help it. Cal and he have a long history together.

"I fall out of touch all the time, and you don't worry about me," Wolf laughs from the back seat as he watches the sand drift past the car.

"You can handle yourself," Brock says over his shoulder. Cal smirks, shaking her head. A comfortable silence fills the car. It only lasts a moment or two before Cal's phone is chirping. She fishes it out of her pocket, answering the video call.

"Hey, William!" She says as the video loads, and she angles the camera, so he can see her and Wolf.

"Hello, lovely people!" William chirps with a giggle. "Who is driving?" He seems momentarily confused.

"Brock," Cal replies, turning the phone slightly, so William can see the driver's seat better.

"Good! I have some news to share with all of you!" William gushes. Wolf leans forward so all three of them are crammed into the frame.

"What's up?" Wolf asks.

"I'm getting married!" William holds up his hand to show off the simple silver band with two sparkling white stones set into it. "Bernd proposed!"

"Congratulations!" Wolf and Cal say in unison. They glance at each other then back at the phone.

"That's wonderful William!" Brock adds.

"When you get home, Cal, we're going to have to get together. We want a fairy tale wedding!" William continues. Bernd leans into the frame, kissing William on the cheek.

"I'll help where I can," Cal smiles, trying very hard to be happy for her friend. Talking about wedding planning with her ex-husband looking over her shoulder is just a mildly uncomfortable situation.

"We'll talk more when we're both stateside, Cal. Love y'all!" William waves and ends the call. Cal tucks the phone back into her pocket. Brock focuses on the traffic, which is thinning out quickly. Wolf sits back in his seat, staring out the window.

"Looks like William is a reformed ho," Wolf chuckles. Brock laughs with him. Cal just smiles softly. She is glad William has found his prince charming, but it makes her look at her own unresolved feelings. Silence envelops the car again as they travel down the road and further into the desert.

"How far out are we going?" She asks, as they drive further into the desert.

"Pretty far out. It's a tomb that was just recently uncovered. The other team pulled out halfway through their dig. I'm not sure why," Brock says with a shrug.

"That's not a good sign," Cal says, whining slightly. "Shit always goes bad when the other team leaves."

"This is why you get all the information before accepting a dig," Wolf says in a teasing sing-song voice.

"Fuck you, Wolf," Cal snaps, shifting in her seat.

"Been there. Done that and I don't plan on going back," Wolf replies, smirking haughtily at the back of her head. Cal just rolls her eyes, ignoring the pain in her soul caused by his words.

"Anyway, this pendant is supposed to bring good fortune and luck to whoever possesses it," Brock interrupts, trying to get the two back on track.

"That doesn't sound like much of a curse," Cal says, glaring at Wolf over her shoulder before focusing her attention on Brock.

"Yeah, I know," Brock pauses to focus on the road as he turns the SUV off the pavement and onto a dirt road. "The problem comes in other aspects. You get a job promotion; your spouse loses their job. You win the lottery, but your house burns down. It's sort of tit-for-tat," Brock shrugs again.

"Still not much of a curse compared to others," Cal repeats, turning her attention back to sand.

"This coming from the Queen of Bad Luck herself," Wolf mutters, not quietly enough. Brock tries to choke back a chuckle and fails. Cal turns slightly, focusing her attention out the passenger side window, trying to ignore the two men. If this keeps up, she is in for a long and miserable trip. All she can see is sand for miles and miles, no signs of anything else.

"Why do these Russian guys want this ankh so bad?" Cal wonders out loud.

"The same reason everyone else wants you to find these random things," Brock glances at her, then turns his attention back to driving.

"Yeah," she mutters, staring off at the horizon. The rich only want these things to say they have them. The actual benefits, or detractors, that came with the artifact didn't matter to them. Cal shifts in her seat, trying to get comfortable. "Are we gonna be on this trail much longer?" She asks, stifling a yawn.

"Yep, I told you the site is a way out there," Brock reminds her.

"Is it all desert? Or are we going to find a town eventually?" Wolf half whines from the backseat, bored already.

"No towns. Just desert for the next," Brock peers at his watch then back out the window, "two hours or so."

Wolf heaves a sigh, flopping back in his seat. This makes Cal laugh. The sand shimmers in the sun. Waves of heat make the horizon dance and waver in front of them. Brock adjusts the AC, trying to keep cool in the heat. Wolf stretches out on the back seat, deciding a nap was better than the awkward silence.

"How've ya been, Brock? I feel like we haven't talked in forever." She turns in her seat, trying to get a better look at her friend.

"Not too bad. I feel like I'm working less with each passing year," Brock says with a shrug. He holds the wheel in one hand and rests the other hand on his leg.

"Come back to work with me. I can use a good, reliable bodyguard," Cal hopes she sounds convincing.

"You had one, after me," Brock shoots her a meaningful glance before focusing back on the desert ahead. "Besides, I can't keep up with you anymore."

"You never had a problem in the past," she says with a knowing smile. "Besides, he's not reliable or useful," Cal stresses the last part.

"You found me useful for something once upon a time," Wolf mutters before Brock can comment. His voice is thick with sleep. Brock's free hand covers his mouth to stifle the laughter that threatens to spill from his lips. Cal rolls her eyes, trying to conceal a smirk. Yes, he was useful once upon a time, but not to her anymore.

Cal stares out the window, watching trees go by in the distance. She assumes it is an oasis. The rest of the ride passes in relatively comfortable silence, other than the occasional joke between Cal and Brock or the occasional snore from Wolf.

"He always sleeps this soundly?" Brock asks as he slows the vehicle down and turns into camp. Cal sees the tents are already up, and a fire pit has been built.

"Yeah, I'm pretty sure he could sleep through a bombing," Cal replies as she unbuckles her seat belt. There is another SUV-type vehicle parked on this side of the camp, which Brock parks behind. An older man leans against the front fender. Cal places him somewhere between seventy and one hundred and seven. He seems out of place, with his white hair slicked back and his yellow lensed aviator glasses. He is dressed in khaki pants and a light blue button-down shirt. Cal notes a slight stoop. Several men are unloading gear from the secondary truck.

"Hey, Stan!" Brock says with a wave out his now open window. The older man waves back. Wolf mutters and grumbles as he sits up.

"We there?" Wolf says with a large yawn.

"We've arrived, sleeping beauty," Brock chuckles. The other driver moves from the hood of the SUV to the driver's seat. Two other men climb into the truck with the older gent. The vehicle starts and it pulls away.

Cal hops out of the car, as do Brock and Wolf. She is the first one at the back of the truck, pulling the hatch up. Cal grabs her backpack and settles it onto her shoulders. She grabs her duffle bag, setting it at her feet. Wolf stretches, then unloads his bags and shuts the trunk. Cal gives Brock a big hug and a kiss on the cheek.

"Take care of yourself, old man," Cal says with a smile.

"You too, kid," Brock replies. He shakes Wolf's hand. Brock climbs back into the Jeep and guides the vehicle out of camp. Cal scans the campsite, seeing several tents are already set up and a few more are going up. Directly behind her campsite is a large oasis. Palm trees create shade, and lower bushes create a bit of cover around the deep spring-fed pools. A deeply tanned, olive-skinned man with ebony hair stands from his seat and makes his way across the campsite. Wolf is busying himself with adjusting his backpack to make it sit more comfortably.

"Doctor and Mister Corrigan?" The man asks, arching one eyebrow.

"It's Doctor Coburn," Cal politely corrects. "Please call me Cal.

"My apologies. And you must be Bryan?" he says, turning to face the bodyguard.

"It's Wolf," he replies with a smile.

"I'm Amir Najjar. I'm your guide." Amir's voice holds a faint accent. He smiles a bright and happy smile. His eyes, chocolate brown, sparkle in the sunlight. He offers his hand;

Cal shakes it before letting her hand drop away. Wolf also shakes the man's hand. "Follow me. Your tent is this way. I apologize, you will be sharing. Mr. Maximov and his employer told me you were married," Amir motions for them to follow, leading the way across the camp toward the tents. These are large white canvas tents, much larger than they are used to.

"We'll manage," Cal says as politely as possible. Amir zips open the tent flap and motions them inside. Thankfully, there are two separate cots. Cal steps inside, pulling one cot to the opposite side of the tent. She drops her duffle bag and backpack to the ground. "Thank you, Amir."

"Please take your time getting settled. Dinner will be ready shortly," Amir smiles, waves, and makes his way back to the shade and the others. Cal sits on her cot, digging a hair tie out of her backpack. She rakes through her hair, pulling it into a ponytail. Wolf pulls his cot farther away from Cal, then sits down to rearrange his equipment. He hands over her ammo, which she takes and sets on the bed next to her. Cal opens her duffle bag, and hands over his 10 MMs in turn. Wolf uses a rag from his bag, wiping them off before he nestles them into his shoulder holsters. The holster is set on top of his bag.

Cal puts away her ammo and slides the duffle bags under her cot. She stands and leaves the tent. Confident footsteps carry her across the camp, toward the rest of the team. Wolf follows silently behind her. Under the canopy sits

Amir, several other Egyptian men, a petite redheaded woman, a tall skinny black-haired man, and a stocky blond man. Cal takes a seat in an empty camp chair, and Wolf sits across from her.

"Everyone, this is Cal and Wolf," Amir says, motioning to them in turn. Cal offers a small wave and Wolf nods to the team.

"I'm Tessa Sims," the redhead smiles as she speaks. "I'll be your medic." Wolf takes in the sight of the medic, which causes Tessa to smile even brighter as she catches the mercenary looking her over.

"I'm Cyprian Vlahos. Everyone calls me Cy. I'm your demolitions guy." The skinny dark-haired man offers a wave to the newcomers.

"Cyprian...Oxide...why do demolition guys always have such oddball names?" Cal interrupts.

"You knew my cousin," Cy's good-natured attitude seems to melt away. "I didn't realize you were that Cal."

"How many Cal's do you know in this line of work?" She asks, looking at him confusedly. Cy doesn't answer her.

"I guess I'm last but not least," the blond grins, trying to lighten the mood. "I'm Bowen. I'll be your rigger for this expedition."

Cal takes a moment to look at each person in turn. She doesn't like not picking her team, but they seem nice enough and hopefully, they're competent. Cal doesn't need to have another bad expedition, like China. Wolf had taken a seat next to the medic. He and Tessa talk quietly. Cal turns her attention to Amir.

"We will head in early in the morning. It's too warm to walk into the tomb today." Amir says. "And night sets fast in the desert."

"Where's the tomb? I just see dirt and the oasis," Cal says, looking around.

"Just past the trees," Amir motions. "Not too far of a walk from here is a small cave-like opening which takes us into the tomb." He motions as he speaks. Cal nods, turning to look over her shoulder toward the oasis before she turns back to the group. Amir's men sit to one side, dressed in lightweight linens. Bowen and Cy are playing tic-tac-toe in the sand. Wolf is talking with Amir now while Tessa organizes a small first aid kit.

"Have any of you worked together before?" Cal asks, causing everyone to turn their eyes toward her.

"I think only my men have," Amir replies. "And, of course, you and Mr. Corrigan...I mean Wolf."

Cal just nods, turning her attention to the oasis. That makes her less comfortable, knowing that very few people have worked together. She wants a team with a good rapport and who can trust each other. This is the last time I take a job like this, Cal thinks. At least there is no tension among the group, aside from what lingers between Wolf and her. Everyone else seems to be at ease with each other. Cal just watches them interact. The sun is sinking on the horizon. Cal's stomach growls. One of Amir's men stands and walks off toward a large tent.

He returns moments later with MREs. Cal winces at the sight of those freeze-dried meals. Amir starts a fire in the pit just outside the canopy they currently sit under. Cal takes one of the freeze-dried meals as it's handed to her. She opens it, setting aside the crackers and candy. Each person prepares their meal, and they fall into easy conversation as they eat. They talk about where they're from and what has brought them there. Cal listens, watching the sunset burn slowly along the horizon. Once the sun slips beneath the dunes, the air takes on the chill. Amri's men take turns stoking the fire.

Cal stands, "night all." She waves, then strides across the dirt to the tent she will be sharing with Wolf. She wants to be able to write in her journal without him lurking around, although she is unsure if he'll be back to their tent. Part of her hopes that he ends up in Tessa's tent. That would make it easier for Cal in a way. On the other hand, every time the medic is near him or touching him, Cal wants to shoot her. She opens the tent, steps inside. She shuts the flap and sits on the edge of the cot. Digging her journal and a pen from her bag, she opens the book and clicks on her lantern.

Cal dates the page, writes down everyone's names and jobs. The first she writes about is the miscommunication with the sleeping arrangement. She writes about Brock, and the drive out to camp. She writes a little about each team member. Cal signs her name to the entry, closes the book, and puts it away. She changes into cotton shorts and a tank top before climbing into bed. Cal turns off the lantern and stretches. Moments later, she is asleep.

When Wolf comes into the tent, he pauses to watch her. She is asleep, curled up on her side with her blanket pulled up to her chin. He reaches over, tugging the corner of the blanket to cover her feet. He changes from his travel clothes to a pair of lightweight sleeping pants. He makes sure the tent is closed and secure before he climbs under the blankets on his cot. He stretches out on his side, facing the doorway. Camp is quiet as the rest of the team makes their way to their tents. Everyone is eager for an early start the next morning.

November 17th

Amir Najjar – Guide

Tessa Sims – Medic

Bowen – Rigger

Cy Vahlos – Demolitions

Wolf – Bodyguard

       I have to share a tent with my ex-husband. Really? I know the divorce just finalized, but we have been separated for months. I have been using my maiden name since I left the cabin. I am just glad they got us two separate cots, or he would be sleeping on the ground. I'm not sharing a bed with him. Sharing my sleeping space is bad enough.

       Brock was our driver out here. It was very nice to see him. I feel like I haven't seen him in months. I missed his hugs. I think when I get back stateside, we have to get together. I really need to mend some bridges I burned when I left Wolf. Brock is still one of my dearest friends. He has known me since I was just a punk college kid. I shouldn't hold Wolf's doings against him. It isn't Brock's fault we didn't work out. We tried. The drive to camp was uneventful, except for the guys picking on me. It felt like old times. It was almost three hours before we reached the site. Three hours from the city to sand to the oasis. Brock headed back right from camp.

Amir is our guide on this trip. He has brought with him a small group of Egyptian men to help with carrying items as well as to translate. He seems nice enough, and eager to work. I think he will work well with our group.

Tessa is the medic. A petite thing, but hopefully what she lacks in size she makes up for in skills. She seems very interested in my bodyguard. I'm torn about that. I want her and Wolf to hit it off, it will make separating from him easier. At the same time, I want them to hate each other. Despite that, she does seem nice.

Bowen is the rigger. He is upbeat and happy. I didn't get to do a lot of talking to him, so I don't have much of an opinion on him.

Cyprian aka Cy is our demolitions guy. I don't think he likes me. He is Oxide's cousin. I feel like he will do his job, but he will not be my friend. If he is half as good as Oxide was, I may have to add him to my contact list.

We are heading toward the tomb tomorrow. Early start to get going before the heat of the day.

-Cal

Chapter 7

The sun is barely peeking over the horizon as the team assembles around the fire pit. Amir has brewed coffee, and everyone is enjoying a mug. Cal and Amir stand to one side, discussing the tomb. She likes to know some of the logistics of where they are going. Amir has a map. It's one of the dreaded hand-drawn maps that are never to scale because there is no scale. Cal internally cringes.

"As far as we can tell, it's only about a quarter explored. The other team left in quite a hurry." Amir says.

"'Cause this place is cursed," mumbles one of Amir's men. Amir glares at the man.

"Don't be superstitious, Selim." Amir snaps before turning back to Cal. "I'm sure the good doctor doesn't have time for stupid superstitions." His voice softens as he speaks of Cal.

"Superstitions come from somewhere. There is usually a tiny grain of truth in them." Cal shrugs.

"No matter how microscopic," Wolf pipes up. Cal rolls her eyes, sipping her coffee. The conversation changes from work to more general topics. No one wants to think about curses associated with the tomb. As breakfast is finished, and the sun is still low on the horizon, everyone heads to their tents to get their gear. Cal strides off, not bothering to see if Wolf is following. She steps through the door of the tent, walking to the side she has deemed hers . The first thing she does is load the pistols before sliding them into her gun belt. She fastens it around her waist. She shifts the belt, making it more comfortable. Next, she picks up her backpack and sets it on the cot. Cal empties it of all the extras like clothes and toiletries. She makes sure to keep her extra climbing gear, as well as her marking tape and journal. The bag is much lighter now as she settles it onto her shoulders. Cal adjusts the straps, making the bag rest more comfortably. She smiles to herself as she makes her way past Wolf and out the door.

Wolf watches her go, having forgotten how attractive those revolvers look on her. It occurs to him, it's probably a weird thing to find attractive, and pushes that idea to the back of his mind. He shrugs on his shoulder holsters, taking the time to adjust them to fit more comfortably. He empties his backpack as well, shouldering it before he leaves the tent. Wolf follows the footprints in the sand to where everyone stands under the shade. Even though the sun is not fully up, the air is already feeling warm and dry.

Once at the water's edge, everyone fills canteens and water skins. Cal takes time to verify her water skin is filled before she slides it into her bag and runs the house through the clips in the strap. She knows better than to go into the desert with little to no water. It's not a mistake she would make again. She takes a moment to look around the oasis, appreciating the cool air around the pool. The others finish their tasks, and everyone starts on the trail to the tomb. It is only about a half-mile, maybe a bit more, from the camp to the tomb entrance. Cal can see now it is not the real entrance, instead, it's a hole blasted in the wall by some uncaring oaf.

She takes a moment to look at the opening before leading the way into the dark. It's much cooler in the tomb, and everyone is relieved by that. She turns to look at the murals damaged by an overzealous demolition person, instead of just looking for the door. From what she knew, thanks to Amir, the first three rooms had been cleared. Cal decides to trust the information. She figures they can always go through those rooms at the end. Cal and Amir lead the way through hallways and rooms. Wolf keeps close to them, with the rest of the team following.

They find themselves at a crossroad, looking to the left and right. Cal leads the team to the left, resting her hands on the butts of her guns as she walks. She slows the pace, not wanting to trip any traps this early in the expedition. Cal looks over the artwork and messages, only able to decipher a few things on sight. The team comes to a large door. They spread out along the wall, looking for something to open it. Wolf finds it, twisting a raised scarab on the wall, which causes the door to slide into the floor. He and Cal take the lead, letting the rest of the team follow them slowly. Wolf keeps an eye on the floor, looking for any odd tiles, while Cal watches the walls. So far, so good. They walk further into the room, and now the team can fan out. Everyone moves carefully along the walls, using their fingers to gently brush away dirt from hieroglyphs. Small nooks and crannies explored. Cal finds a small carving of Horus and another of Anubis. Wolf finds a carved scarab about the size of his hand. There is no mention of the ankh in this room at all.

Cal leads the way out of the room, and back down the hall. All the artifacts have been tucked in her bag. They continue past the entrance hall and head toward the other end. The hall seems to stretch forever, disappearing into the darkness. Cal keeps her eyes forward, only glancing to the walls and floor occasionally. She doesn't want to trip, but she also doesn't want to miss any openings. They find two small rooms on either side of the hall. The team splits up, looking through the rooms. There is nothing but murals and hieroglyphs. They move out of the rooms and continue down the hall, hoping to find something of interest. It doesn't look promising, though. Cal has to remind herself that they're still early in the dig.

They step into another large room, this one with several tunnels branching off it. There are several paintings and this time, there are images of the ankh. Cal takes time to photograph each of these images. Amir and his men translate some of the hieroglyphics. Cal pulls out her journal, jots down translations on a back page, and takes photos of the images that match the words. The book is latched and tucked back into her bag. She settles the bag on her shoulders and takes the map from Amir. The room they're in is sketched on the map. Cal adds the tunnels, only sketching out short sections for now. She strides down the hall to her left.

Wolf scrambles after her as the rest of the team is left examining the room, "Hey! Wait up!" He yells, noticing she barely slows down to allow him to catch up. He falls into step beside her. "That's how ya get hurt," he comments.

Cal just shrugs, looking from the floor to the walls and back again. The walls are smooth, with no artwork or hieroglyphics. The floor is covered in soft sand, just deep enough to leave footprints, but not deep enough to cause issues with their footing. They walk along, pausing every once in a while to add to the map. They can no longer hear the rest of the team. Cal isn't even sure if they'll be waiting for them to return. The hallway opens into a large room. She and Wolf both fumble for their bags, looking for flashlights, only to find they have forgotten them. Cal pulls her phone out, clicking open the flashlight application. She turns, scanning the walls with the bright white light. Wolf joins her. They find a large mural depicting the ankh in a sarcophagus. The two of them turn to each other, eyes wide. This is the first time any of the murals have depicted the ankh in more than passing. They both start back the way they had come, jogging in the soft sand. The flashlight bounces off the sand and the walls. Wolf slides to a stop with Cal right behind him. The team turns, surprised by their sudden reappearance.

"We found it!" Cal exclaims. "Well, we found reference to it," she explains.

"Where?" Amir seems excited as he takes a step toward Wolf and Cal.

"This way," Wolf says, leading the way down the dark tunnel. Cal falls into step beside him. The rest of the team follows them, moving quickly. Wolf and Cal talk quietly and excitedly at the head of the team.

It's like old times, like those early digs. The two of them were excited about a find, new information for the history books. It's all wonderful. The whole team spills into the large room, looking around. Flashlights are produced from several bags. Wolf uses his cell phone flashlight, as does Cal, never having shut hers off. The whole room is illuminated by various light sources. Cal stands in the center of the room, spinning in a slow circle. She takes in the whole continuous funeral displayed in one mural.

"Can you believe this?" Cal asks. Wolf has moved to stand next to her.

"No, this is amazing." Wolf is genuinely in awe. Everyone is.

"This portrays the burial of the owner of this tomb. When we find his resting place, we'll find the pendant." Amir says, his voice hushed and reverent.

"We don't know who is buried here?" Cal says, eyebrows raised.

"No. It has been a mystery for some time. Unfortunately, many of these old tombs have been buried for so long no one remembers who is buried where. Until we find the name cartouche, we will not know who is entombed here. If we find it." Amir says.

Cal nods, looking around the room again. Slowly, she takes photos of the mural, planning on piecing them together when she returns home. The rest of the team has taken a walk around the room, admiring the work. Now they make their way back down the hall, with Cal and Wolf bringing up the rear. One of the other hallways would have to bring them closer to their final destination. The team spreads out again in the larger room, letting Cal and Wolf take the lead. Cal heads toward the next tunnel with Wolf walking at her side. The others fall into step behind them. Selim mutters something about curses under his breath, only to be silenced by a sharp word from Amir. Cal ignores the two, but glances at Wolf, who just gives her a faint nod.

"Just like China," he says with a smirk. Cal grunts. She doesn't need another trip like that. It was the last cursed artifact they had gone looking for, and nothing good had come of that trip. They had lost several good men, and at least two others had left severely damaged. The adventurers walk on. Cal makes a mental note to talk to Selim when they return to camp. This hall seems to narrow as they walk. The sand gives way to stone. Cal and Wolf turn their attention from the walls to the floor and back. Neither of them wants to walk into a pit or step on a trap. Too many men and women have been lost like that in the past.

So far, they've just found a long, narrow path. Just when they feel like they're getting nowhere, the hall widens then opens into a large circular room. Pillars and decorative vase-like containers dot the room. Statues of various Egyptian gods sit in the corners, looking down at the team. It gives the room a foreboding feeling. Again, the team spreads out, looking over the various artworks. Cy puts as much space between himself and Cal as he can, working across the room from her.

Wolf takes a few of the men to another wall, looking over some hieroglyphics and a few images of the ankh. The men, in slightly broken English, tell Wolf the story of the ankh. They have seen this on several walls since finding the burial mural. The men with Wolf tell him, the story goes on to say the ankh is buried with the Pharaoh because he didn't want the curse passed on to anyone else. It had taken the man's sons as well as two daughters. At least that is what the story says. Wolf scoffs at the idea.

"Heed these words," one of the men says, looking at Wolf with worry on his face.

"Superstitions don't phase me. Never have and never will." Wolf smirks. "We'll find the ankh, turn it over to the Russians, get paid, and then it's their problem," he says calmly.

Either the words or Wolf's attitude seem to strike a chord with Selim. He pushes past Amir, closing the distance between him and Wolf. A knife appears from thin air and is lifted above his head. Cal turns, seeing this happening in slow motion. She unholsters one pistol, leveling it and squeezing off a single round. The blast echoes through the chamber. The smell of gunpowder fills the room, and one portion of the artwork is obliterated as the bullet slams into it. Smoke curls from the barrel. Selim collapses to the ground, blood pooling around him. Everyone turns. She watches as a few of the men and Tessa run to attend to him.

"He's dead." Tess proclaims as she feels for a pulse. She looks at Cal, narrowing her eyes. "You didn't have to kill him."

"Sorry, toots. I was taught to shoot to kill," Cal holsters her revolver. "If anyone is going to kill Wolf, it's going to be me," she adds.

"Thanks, I think," he says with a shaky voice.

"Don't mention it." She replies. Turning back to the wall, Cal resumes looking over the art. The men talk hurriedly with Amir. Cal ignores them. Until Amir appears on her right side.

"The men would like to take Selim and leave," he says. "They wish to be relieved of this assignment."

"Fine. Let them go. As long as I have the map, we'll be fine." She looks at Amir as she speaks. "You let them know I only killed him to protect one of my own. I've known Wolf far too many years to let someone with a stupid fear kill him." Her voice is sharp. Amir turns, speaks briefly to his men, then turns back to Cal.

"They will return to camp for the night. At first light, they will take Selim's body back to Cairo." Amir nods. "I understand why you did it. I apologize for Selim. He was hot-headed."

"Being hot-headed will get you killed, at least that is what they keep telling me," Cal replies. She offers a sad smile, which he returns before walking back to his men. Cal turns back to Wolf, who has been watching this whole exchange. Slowly, he makes his way across the room to her.

"Thanks." He says again, more genuinely this time.

"Don't mention it. Ever." Cal says and turns back to the wall she was working on. She focuses on her work, feeling eyes boring into her. She does her best to ignore the feeling, but it's hard. Wolf moves to stand next to her, looking over the hieroglyphics. They work in tense silence, dusting years of the grime away from the carved images. Cal pulls her phone from her pocket, taking photos as they go. The rest of the team keeps their distance from Cal and Wolf. One of the men pulls a blanket from his bag and spreads it out on the ground. The men gently lift Selim into the blanket, then lift it by its corners. They make their way out of the room, backtracking their steps toward the exit. Cal watches them go, wondering how many more of the team would join, them before she turns back to the path ahead of them.

They walk along the walls, finding a narrow opening. Cal undoes her gun belt, handing it to Wolf before turning sideways. It's a slow shimmy, but Cal manages to squeeze through the narrow hallway into a small room, no bigger than a closet. Cal takes a moment to look around, even though she can just turn in place. There isn't any room to move. She takes a few photos, then squeezes her way back out of the opening. Cal shows the photos to Amir and Wolf.

"Besides the artwork, it's empty," she shrugs before tucking the phone away and walking back toward the entrance. Once in the doorway, she turns to look the room over again. Besides the footprints, the only change is the deep red staining on the light sand. She leads the team back toward the main room. So far, this tomb has been easy to navigate, but she knows it may not stay that way. Hidden somewhere there could be a maze of tunnels just waiting for the explorers to get lost in. Cal decides they had plenty of time to explore more tomorrow. After what has happened with Wolf and Selim, she decides it will be healthier for them to call it early. The walk to the exit is slow, motivation seemingly zapped from everyone.

They emerge from the tomb and into the hot desert air. The sun beats down on them as Cal leads the way back to camp, barely pausing at the oasis. Amir joins his men under the canopy, while Cal heads off to her tent. Wolf looks down at the gun belt he carries, rolling his eyes.

"You want these?" Wolf asks as he follows her, holding the guns out.

"Oh yeah. Thanks for carrying them," she slides them under her cot, on top of the backpack. She rummages in her bag, pulling out a change of clothes and a towel. Cal leaves the tent, and heads toward the oasis, she doesn't care if Wolf is following her.

Once behind the bushes, Cal looks over the oasis, finding it has two pools, the larger spring-fed one where they had filled their water bottles, and a smaller deep pool filled with a small waterfall. Cal moves to the smaller pool, glad to see it has better coverage from prying eyes. She sets her clean clothes and towel down on a flat rock, stripping out of her dusty travel clothes. Cal wades into the water, pausing as her body adjusts to the cool water. After a few brief moments, she wades deeper and deeper until she is almost chest deep. Cal closes her eyes, letting the water wash away the day's events. She dunks herself under and waits until her lungs burn for her before she surfaces, wiping water from her eyes. As she blinks to clear her vision, Cal is not surprised to see Wolf sitting on a rock near the water.

"Can I help you?" She asks, running her fingers through her hair.

"Just doing my job," he says, with his eyes focused on the horizon. He doesn't dare look at her, for fear of falling deeper in love with her.

"I'll be fine," she grumbles, splashing water on her face.

"You said that in China," he smirks, "and LA." Now his eyes lock with hers.

"That's a low blow, Wolf," she says, turning her back on him. He can see just one of her scars. The one from the drive-by in LA. "Maybe I should have let him gut you," she mutters before she dips under the water again. When she surfaces and turns, it's just in time to see him pull his shirt over his head. In the last few months, a few new scars have been added to his collection, as has a large shoulder tattoo. The black tribal pattern forms an angular wolf's profile with a closed eye.

"I see you added a douchebag breakup tattoo," Cal comments.

"Isn't that what you're supposed to do when the woman you planned to spend the rest of your life with leaves you?" Wolf rolled his eyes as he spoke.

"When you're a douche, yeah it is," she responded sharply.

"I'm sorry. I guess this is harder than I thought," he motions from her to him and back again.

"Then let's lay some ground rules," she says as she emerges from the water and grabs her towel. Wolf's eyes travel up her body until the two of them lock eyes. She is smirking, "First off, no more babysitting me while I bathe," she dries off as she talks. The towel is wrapped around her. "Second, no more of that." She motions to his shirtless torso. "Lastly, I'm not going to save you again." Cal drops the towel and quickly dresses.

"Fine, I can agree to most of that," Wolf says as he strips out of his clothes in front of her before he wades into the water.

"Why only most of it?" She says, after a momentary pause to enjoy the sight of a very naked Wolf.

"I'm your bodyguard. I go where you go. And, well, we always save each other Cal. It's how this has always worked," Wolf says before sinking under the water. She mutters to herself, turning on her heel, and strides back toward camp. Wolf surfaces just in time to see her storm through the trees.

Part of her knows he is right. They always save each other. It's how their relationship has always worked and will always work. Cal grabs an MRE, a mug of hot water, then heads to her tent. There is no point in sitting with a team that now hates her. She will not be surprised if they are all packed up and gone by the morning. Cal opens the package, pulling the contents out and setting them on the bed. Cal takes her time to make her food. It's instant chili, but it's better than nothing. She eats the food quietly, listening to the few snippets of conversation that reaches her. It sounds mostly like Amir's men. Outside the closed tent door, she hears movement. Cal leans over, gently sliding one of her pistols from its holster. Tessa, Bowen, and Cy all lean in the doorway.

"Mind if we join you?" Bowen asks, timidly.

"It's not super friendly out there," Tessa adds with a small smile. Cy lingers behind the two. He doesn't want to be in either place.

"Sure," Cal shrugs, settling the gun back into its holster, then resuming eating. The group walks through the door, sitting on a loose circle in the center of the tent.

"Where's Wolf?" Tessa asks, a bit too eagerly for Cal's liking.

"Bathing," she snaps. Bowen and Cy glance at each other.

"Sorry," Tessa mutters, nibbling a piece of jerky.

"So, Cal, are you ok? I mean after today..." Bowen asks, trying not to sound like he is prying.

"Not the first guy she's shot," Wolf's voice comes from the tent doorway. He also has an MRE in hand and skirts around the group, so he can sit on his cot.

"Really? You make a habit out of that?" Tessa sounds disgusted to be working with someone who has killed.

"Only when you try to kill me, people I like or someone annoys me," Cal smiles. It's an overly sweet smile that unnerves Tessa.

"You like me! You really like me!" Wolf exclaims as he finishes making his meal. The team laughs loudly.

"Don't flatter yourself, Wolf," Cal rolls her eyes, finishing her dinner. Tessa watches the two, looking from Wolf and Cal and back again.

"You guys known each other long?" Cy asks, shifting to sit cross-legged on the tent floor.

"A few years," Wolf answers before Cal can.

"I think the question is how well do they know each other," Tessa mutters, drawing all eyes to her. She blushes faintly.

"Jealous much?" Cal says with an arrogant smile.

"We know each other biblically, you could say," Wolf rolls his eyes at Cal. This makes Tessa's blush deepen.

"That's why we're stuck sharing the tent. Nothing like working with your ex-husband," Cal shrugs and chuckles. Tessa almost visibly relaxes at this idea. She feels like she no longer has to worry about coming between the two of them. Cal sets her trash on the floor of the tent next to her cot. The conversation dissolves from Cal and Wolf to more general topics such as hobbies. Bowen and Cy are looking at pictures of Wolf's gun collection.

"Do you think we'll find it?" Tessa's voice startles Cal. She looks at the medic.

"Who knows. It looks like it exists, so that's something. Many of these tombs have been gutted of valuables. If we find the burial room, there is a very good chance we won't find the ankh or anything else." Cal shrugs. It's a bit brutal, but it is the truth. Many of the times Cal has been sent out on digs like these, it's a wild goose chase. Cal watches the boys talk guns then looks back at Tessa. "First time in Egypt?"

"Yeah. I've always wanted to come here, but never got picked for a job. How about you?" She responds.

"Been here lots of times." Cal shrugs. "I don't think there are many countries I haven't been to at this point," she smirks, staring out the open tent flaps across the camp. The sun is low on the horizon, starting to set. Tessa watches the boys sharing photos while Cal stares across the camp.

"Cal has a few decent pieces herself," Wolf says. The words bring her out of her stupor. She turns and looks at him, mildly confused.

"Did you just compliment my firearms?" Cal asks with a quiet laugh.

"For antiques, they're nice," Wolf laughs.

"Don't talk bad about my antiques. They saved your ass today," Cal reminds him, shifting on her cot. She tucks her legs under her, watching as the other men file off to sleep, the fire has burned down to glowing embers. Cy yawns, and waves as he leaves the tent. He wanders off to his tent. Bowen and Tessa follow shortly after. It's not long before the sky is dark, and the stars sparkle brightly overhead. Cal and Wolf sit in silence, looking out at the desert before them.

Without a word, Cal stands and closes the tent doors. She makes sure the door is secure before returning to her cot. She sits down, looking at Wolf. "I think Ms. Tessa has a wee crush on you dear," Cal chuckles.

Wolf rolls his eyes, turning his back to her as he changes into light cotton sleep pants, and leaving his shirt off. Cal takes this chance to change into her PJs herself. She is just pulling her tank top down over her stomach as Wolf turns around. He catches sight of the scars and the small tattoo on her abdomen.

"When did you get that?" He asks, tipping his head to one side.

"None of your business," she replies coolly, smoothing the shirt over the tattoo. It's their son's initials with small angel wings. Just a simple, little tribute to the life that never got to happen.

"Can we talk?" Wolf asks, making a small attempt. "About us?" He says, smiling. Cal looks at him, unimpressed with his choice of topic.

"What is there to talk about? When we were good, we were good. Everything just went to shit real fast. You left me, as soon as you knew I would survive." Cal says. "You left Brock, William and me to plan the funeral. You left them to care for me after promising to take care of *our* family. You came home long enough to see my son buried. Have you even been back to see the headstone?" Her head tips to one side, and she fights to keep from yelling.

"Have you?" Wolf snaps back. "I'm not the only one who made mistakes. Instead of us trying to fix things, you threw yourself into work. Have you been to see him recently?" He repeats the stinging question.

"We really fucked this up," Cal says with a sigh. "We fucked it all up." She rests her elbows on her knees, and her head in her hands. Neither of them speak as they both fight back tears. Cal looks up, locking eyes with Wolf. They are both hurting, but neither of them can continue with the conversation for fear of breaking down in front of the other.

Cal climbs under her blankets, laying with her back to him. She listens as he settles into his bed. It's not long before Wolf's breathing slows, and he is asleep. Cal lays in her cot, just listening to him. His steady breathing lulls her to sleep, as it had so many times during their whirlwind relationship.

A few hours later, Cal bolts upright in bed. She bites back a scream, her hands reaching for her abdomen. She pants, and her heart hammers in her chest as she looks around in fear. As she recognizes the tent and the smell of the desert air. She relaxes back onto the cot.

November 18th

      I shot a man today. One of Amir's men. He tried to kill Wolf. I wasn't about to have him kill my bodyguard. Besides, if anyone is going to kill my ex it's going to be me.

      Amir's men are leaving tomorrow. They no longer want to work with me. If they were worried about the job or the artifact going to the Russians, they shouldn't have come on the job. Oh, well. I won't be surprised if we're the only two left at camp tomorrow.

      We haven't found anything of importance yet. Hopefully, we will soon. I hate uneventful digs. I just want the artifact and to head home. I need to get space between me and Wolf.

      Speaking of Wolf, he got a tattoo. It's a black tribal looking shoulder piece made to look like the profile of a, you guessed it, a wolf. Its eye is closed. It's a douchebag break up tattoo, and he admitted it!

      No more digs without getting a full list of employees from now on.

      Wolf and I had a fight tonight. He wanted to try to talk about us, and fix things. It just turned into us yelling at each other. I almost felt like I was back in Wyoming again. I may pack up and leave with Amir's men in the morning.

I can't deal with the fighting or the tension. I hate this. I hate that I still love him.

-Cal

Chapter 8

The sun is just peeking over the horizon when the bespectacled driver appears in the camp. Amir's men carefully load Selim's body into the large SUV with their gear stacked around him. They climb into the vehicle. Cal emerges from the tent, just in time to see them leave. She watches the truck until it's just a speck in a large cloud of dust. She walks across the fire pit, tossing some logs into it. After a bit of rummaging, she finds paper and matches, with a bit of effort, Cal gets a decent fire going. She takes the percolator to the oasis and fills it with water. There is a pause as she stops at the kitchen area and puts coffee grounds in the filter before putting the lid on it. She takes it over the fire, only mildly surprised to find Wolf sitting next to it.

Cal tries to ignore him as she takes a seat across from him. Her eyes focus on the fire. The remaining team members slowly make their way from their tents to the fire. All of Amir's men have left, leaving only Amir, Tessa, Bowen, and Cy besides Wolf and Cal. She had done expeditions with smaller teams and honestly is surprised more of them didn't leave.

Cal pours herself a cup of coffee, then returns to look over camp. Her eyes wander back to the team. No matter what, it's a depressing sight. As everyone wakes up, and caffeine flows through their veins, a low murmur of conversation starts. She just listens. Wolf moves to sit next to her, on the left. Amir sits on the other side of her.

"We'll head back down after everyone has finished breakfast," Cal says quietly. She drinks the last of her coffee, then stands. Everyone watches as she walks back to her tent. Amir and Wolf exchange glances, then Wolf stands and goes after Cal as she disappears into the tent.

He pushes through the tent flap, to find Cal sitting on the edge of her cot with her head in her hands. She doesn't look up at him right away. Wolf approaches her slowly, not wanting to be a second casualty on this trip. As his shadow falls over Cal, she looks up at him. Her eyes glint fiercely, even with teardrops threatening to spill over her lids and down her cheeks. The fight with Wolf from the night before, shooting Selim, the loss of half their team, all of it has caught up with the woman.

Wolf doesn't bother to think, instead, he sits next to her. His arms envelop her, pulling her close to him. Cal finds herself leaning into him, breathing deeply. As had happened in the burger joint parking lot, it takes Cal's brain, body, and heart a few minutes to get on the same page. Cal pushes Wolf away, fumbling her pen out of her journal. She wraps her hand around the writing implement, swinging it toward Wolf.

The point sinks into the meaty part of his forearm. Cal pulls the pen back, jumping to her feet. Wolf stares at her, blood trickling down his arm. "You stabbed me! Why the fuck?!" He looks down at his arm, watching the blood, "You lunatic! You fucking stabbed me!"

"I told you to keep your fucking hands off me!" Cal yells back. She grabs her gun belt, and backpack before storming out of the tent. The yelling has brought the rest of the team across the camp to the large tent. Cal brushes past them as they lean in the door. Tessa spots the blood running down his arm and dripping onto the floor. She jogs off to her tent.

"That crazy," he pauses, taking a deep breath. "She stabbed me with a pen. Who the hell uses a pen?" Wolf mutters. Tessa squeezes between Cy and Bowen, first aid kit in hand. She sits next to him, taking his arm. The medic opens the kit, pulling out gauze and peroxide. Tessa wipes the blood away, cleaning the wound. She puts a gauze pad over the injury, wrapping it with an ace wrap. Once Wolf is taken care of, the rest of the team heads off to grab their gear. They meet with Amir by the fire, which he has put out. Cal is nowhere to be seen.

"Where's Cal?" Wolf asks, looking around.

"She said she'd meet us inside," he motions toward the oasis and tomb beyond.

"That's a bad idea. She's not in a good mood. I don't know what's going on in her head," Wolf mutters as he leads the team toward the tomb. Everyone hurries to keep up with him.

"She just stabbed you, and you're worried about her?" Cy seems confused.

"Cal is not ok. I'm not sure what is happening to her. Between the shooting yesterday and what she went through last year, I think we have a problem." Wolf doesn't give them any more than that. The team falls silent as they walk through the oasis and toward the entry of the burial site. Wolf leads the way into the tomb, and toward the room of tunnels. Cal is waiting for them there, seeming much calmer now. She looks at Wolf, then turns her eyes to the map. Wolf catches what may be a glimpse of guilt in that momentarily glance.

"I told you I'd wait," she says, voice barely above a whisper. "Everyone ready?" Cal looks up again, purposefully avoiding looking at Wolf. They all nod. She turns and starts down a tunnel they hadn't explored. Cal references the map, occasionally adding to the drawing. They emerge into another small room with several more tunnels spreading out from it. Cal adds the room and the start of the tunnels. "Which way Amir?" She asks.

"I would start here and work our way around." He says, motioning to the far-right tunnel. Cal nods, following his advice. She leads the way down the tunnel directly to her right. She walks slowly, not wanting to trip any traps. Wolf joins her, not saying anything. The hall ends very abruptly, causing everyone to bump into each other as Cal and Wolf stop quickly.

"Well then," Wolf mutters, hesitantly touching the wall. "Looks like it's just a wall, that is weird." Cal looks around the hallway, as everyone does. They don't see anything but the surrounding walls. The team turns around and walks back the way they came. Cal quickly sketches the hall on the map. Once back in the room of hallways, they start down the next hall. This one is wider and taller. Cal and Wolf keep a slow pace as they make their way deeper into the tomb. The hall seems to descend ever so slightly. The dirt floor gives way to stone.

They move slower now, both to check for traps, and so Cal can add to the map. The hall opens into a large room, with artwork all over the walls and pillars from the floor to the ceiling. Wolf motions to a circle of stones on the floor. Cal walks over to it, tapping it with the toe of her boot. It crumbles into a well.

"Watch the floors. We have traps," Cal says.

"I see you've learned since China," Wolf smirks. Cal looks at him, smiling softly. They move to look at the mural on one wall while the rest of the team looks the other walls over. "Be careful what you touch," Wolf says over his shoulder, catching Bowen with his hand in midair. Bowen drops his hand to his side.

They work in tense silence, with Cal taking the occasional photo on the wall. There are a few doorways, but no one dares go through them yet. Finally, Cal turns to Wolf and takes a deep breath. "I'm sorry about well," she motions to his arm. Her eyes turn to her feet. "I don't know what happened."

"Some part of your brain said 'Stab Wolf. It'll be fun'." Wolf replies, trying to lighten the mood. "I'm sorry I touched you. I just wanted to comfort you. You looked so scared and angry."

"I know. I shouldn't have reacted like I did. This just isn't easy," Cal says with a shrug. Wolf smirks, mimicking her shrug.

Cal nods and turns back to what she was working on. Behind them, a yell and loud twang causes them to turn around. Bowen stands, shirt sleeve pinned to the wall. A guilty look is plastered on his face. A crossbow bolt holds him in place, Cal and Wolf exchange a look.

"It's China all over again," she mutters, striding over to the man. "What is with your riggers touching things you're not supposed to?" Cal growls at him, yanking the bolt from the wall.

"When I say don't touch anything, I mean it!" Wolf says sternly. "Cal and I have lost too many good men because they didn't listen," Wolf shakes his head, turning back to where he and Cal had been working. Cal slides the bolt into Bowen's bag as a reminder.

"Hands to yourself. I don't want anyone else to die," Cal lectures Bowen before returning to Wolf's side. Instead of returning to work, she steps partway into the doorway and shines her flashlight toward the ceiling. She is relieved to see it is solid. Cal adds the doorways to the map, before moving to check the next one. Egyptians often hung boulders in doorways to drop on grave robbers. Cal looks up at the ceiling of the second door, finding a boulder looming overhead. She carefully leaves the doorway, sketching a faint X on the map. She repeats this process with the next two doorways and finds only one more boulder. Cal marks this on the map, before turning to her team. "We have two safe doorways and two not-so-safe doorways. The next question is, are the trapped doorways the hallways that would lead to treasure, or is it a red herring?" She looks to Amir for answers.

"Your guess is as good as mine," Amir shrugs. "There is not always rhyme or reason behind these traps." Cal then looks at Wolf, her voice of reason and logic.

"Let's hit the safe ones first, then we can check out the other ones," Wolf suggests. The others nod.

"Lunch first?" Cal asks. The team nods. They stand in a loose circle, with their bags at their feet. Various field friendly foods like trail mix, and jerky, are pulled from various pouches. It's not a filling lunch but it will fuel them through the rest of the dig.

"That sounds like a good idea. Wolf, Bowen, and Tessa go through the first doorway. I'll take Amir and Cy through the next one. Please be careful. Document everything you can and grab any artifacts that may be found." They all nod and disperse to their teams. Cal and Wolf glance at each other before leading their teams down their hallways.

It's a narrow hallway, with a stone floor. Wolf must lead them single file farther into the tomb. It's plain with no hieroglyphics or paintings. Wolf looks around, trying to keep an eye out for any traps. The team walks close together. The narrow path opens into a wide room, but half of it is filled with sand. The trio spreads out, skirting around the sand and stone, to explore the rest of the room. There are a few paintings on the walls and another raised scarab. Wolf wiggles it, figuring since the last one opened a door, this one should too. Nothing happens. Everyone takes photos, while Wolf pokes around in the sand and rubble.

Cal's hallway is also plain, but with a stone floor. It's a slow walk but no one complains, after all no one wants to trip a trap and get hurt or die. Everyone follows in the footsteps of the person in front of them.

"Why did you stab Wolf?" Cy asks, quickly regretting it.

"I can't answer that, Cy. We have a complicated relationship. We can work well together, but for the most part, I hate him," she shrugs. "I know that makes no sense, but it's how it is."

"But you saved his life, then you stabbed him?" Cy presses.

"I told you it's complicated," Cal says sharply.

"Let it go, Cyprian," Amir tries to calm the situation. Cy turns his attention to his feet. The team continues in silence.

"Can I ask you about Oxide?" Cy finally says. "I'd like to know how he died."

"He saved our lives. Some men turned on us and were trying to kill us. Oxide, as quick thinking as he was, threw some explosives into the tunnel. When they went off, he was too close to the blast." Cal doesn't look at Cy, keeping her attention on the path. The hallway splits off into two hallways. Cal stops, turning to Amir and Cy. "Looks like we get to head back. There's no way we're splitting up any further. We'll have to bring the rest of the team down here to explore the two tunnels." She motions for them to turn back around, which the two reluctantly do. The trio hikes back down the hall, meeting up with the rest of their team.

"Found anything good?" Cal asks, looking at Bowen, Tessa, and Wolf.

"A half-collapsed room." Wolf shrugs. "You?"

"More tunnels. Gonna need all of us to head down, so we can check out both tunnels." Cal motions for them to follow her as she speaks. Everyone stretches out in a single file line, walking in silence as Cal leads them farther into the tomb. Once they reach the split tunnels, Cal stops and turns to the team. She stands in front of the left-hand tunnel. Wolf points to the right tunnel. Cy and Tessa follow him. Cal leads Amir and Bowen down her tunnel.

As they walk, Wolf pokes at random odd-looking stones. Only to find they are just rocks. The hallway seems to continue straight forever before taking a turn and opening to a large circular room. In the center of the room is another circle, this one made out of a low wall. Wolf walks to it, leaning over to find a dark tunnel. His lamp barely penetrates the shadows. Cy and Tessa join him.

"Weird place for a well," Tessa says.

"Well of Souls, maybe?" Cy jokes, looking at the medic.

"I wonder how deep it goes," Wolf says. "Looks like Bowen gets to show off his rigging skills for Cal." Wolf glances around the room. The walls once were painted with a bright mural, but it has faded to almost nothingness over the years.

"Let's go get the others. Cal will want to see this," Wolf takes the lead, heading back toward where they had separated from the others.

Down the other hallway, Cal leads her team along the trail. As they walk, it seems to get narrower and narrower. Although she is not normally claustrophobic, Cal feels a bit tense, which only gets worse as the walls get closer.

"Maybe we should turn back," Bowen's voice shakes slightly as he speaks. Amir chuckles from the rear of the group.

"Not until we see where this goes," Cal says. She doesn't want to betray her feelings to her team. The hall has narrowed considerably by now. Cal's shoulders brush against the uneven walls. Just when Cal is sure the walls will close in completely, they step into a large room, dotted with sarcophagi. None of them are overly fancy, like royalty, but they are still very ornate. Amir walks to the center coffin. He looks it over, fingers running over the writing.

"Servants, beloved ones," he says, moving toward his right. Cal moves toward the left, counting as she walks. "And pets." He adds as he finds a few smaller burial plots.

"I count twelve sarcophagi, at least the human-sized ones," Cal calls to Amir.

"And six smaller ones," Amir adds.

"What's this?" Bowen asks, standing near a slanted walkway with a large door at the end.

"Supplies for the afterlife. Food, drinks, money, and the like." Amir says as he joins Bowen.

Cal strides over to join them. In her excitement, she isn't watching the floor. A low rumble fills the room, causing the trio to look around. The floor beneath Cal gives way, and she drops into a pit. Cal cusses and coughs as she waves dust out of her face. Amir and Bowen turn around, confused as to where their leader has gone.

"Cal?" Amir asks into the darkness.

"Down here. In a fucking pit. I fucking hate pits. Hate them." She hollers up to them. Bowen walks over, looking over the edge. *At least the rigger is here,* she thinks, shrugging up at the man.

Bowen steps back, setting his bag down. Cal can hear rummaging and the clink of carabiners. Thankfully, the walls are rough, and she will be able to find hand, and footholds if necessary. A harness and ropes come over the edge of the pit, Bowen leans over again.

"Ready when you are," he calls down. Cal steps into the harness, adjusting it. Around the guns, it's not always easy, but she makes it work. Cal tugs at the ropes, double-checking her connections.

"I'm ready," Cal says, taking a deep breath. Amir and Bowen start pulling, Cal starts climbing. It's slow-going, but finally, they get Cal over the edge of the Well. Wolf and the others emerge into the room as Cal is pulling herself over the edge of the pit.

"Another one? Reminds me of Peru," Wolf laughs.

"Fuck you, Wolf," Cal rolls her eyes as she steps out of the harness and hands the climbing gear to Bowen.

"You name the time and place," Wolf says, from a safe distance. The pen incident is still fresh in his mind. Tessa looks from Wolf to Cal and back again.

"What're you doing here? Aren't you supposed to be exploring the other tunnel?" Cal snaps, turning to face Wolf fully now.

"We did and walked back to the room. You were taking too long," Wolf says with a nonchalant shrug. "You found something cool, I see." He scans the room, taking in the sight.

"Yeah. Did you find anything?" Cal crosses her arms over her stomach, raising her eyebrows.

"We found a well. Much deeper than that one," Wolf says, motioning to the pit she had climbed from. "But you have the rigger."

"Let's go," Cal motions for him to lead the way. Wolf starts back up the pathway, with everyone following in a single file behind him. Cal keeps close to Wolf, he leads them into the tomb, back to the room with the deep well. The small team circles around it. Cal leans forward, looking down. She is not surprised to see inky blackness. Cal is startled when a hand grabs her gun belt. She looks over her shoulder, seeing Wolf standing there. Cal rights herself, moving to sit on the wall of the well, with her feet dangling into the abyss.

"It always makes me so nervous when you do that," Wolf mutters, watching her.

"I'm not your problem anymore." She smirks at him.

Bowen sets his bag down, pulling his gear out of his bag again. He steps into his harness, adjusting the straps. He clips his gear bags to his belt, then starts hammering in his first point. The team watches as he works his way down the wall, soon he disappears into the darkness. Cal turns and stands off the wall. Bowen's light is seen before he is, twinkling like a lonely star in the night's sky. He swings himself over the wall, unclipping from the ropes.

"It's a really deep well. We may want to come down tomorrow." Bowen glances at his watches, checking the time. Everyone nods. They start back up the hallway, talking quietly about the finds. Cal keeps to herself, leading the team over the tomb and mulling over the events of the morning. The sun is setting as they all emerge into the sands. She blinks, looking at the horizon.

Cal leads the way back to camp. Once there, Amir and Cy get the fire going. Cal notices a pile of boxes under the canopy. She walks over to it. On one of the smaller boxes is a note that reads: *Supplies for the next few days. This box is for you. – Brock.*

Cal takes the box and makes her way to the campfire. She sits down, opening the box. Inside are two jars of crystal-clear liquid. Cal grins and tosses the box into the fire.

"Gifts from Brock?" Wolf asks, sitting next to her.

"Yeah, some fire starter," she opens one of the jars, taking two big gulps. The liquid burns its way down her throat to her stomach, where warmth blossoms through her body. She loves every moment of it. The jar is handed off to Wolf, who takes a long drink before passing it off.

"Be careful. It's strong," Wolf warns as Cy takes the jar.

Cy takes a sip, then hands it off. Amir takes a decent haul of the liquid, then passes it off. Both Tessa and Bowen only sip the liquid. Tessa's face wrinkles as she sticks her tongue out.

"What is that?" Tessa rasps, wiping tears from her eyes.

"Brock's special recipe," Cal grins, taking a long drink from the container. She shivers, goosebumps rising along her arms. She holds the jar out for anyone else, only Wolf takes her up on the offer. He takes two long gulps, before handing it back to Cal, who takes another swig before capping it. She sets the bottle next to her, looking at the team.

"Tastes like paint thinner," Bowen makes a face.

"I'm sure it could double as paint thinner," Wolf laughs, holding his hand out for the bottle again.

"It does double as a fire starter," Cal hands Wolf the bottle as she speaks. He takes another drink then passes it back.

"Ew," Tessa winces again. Amir grabs a few MREs from the boxes and hands them around. Everyone fixes their dinner, eating and talking. Wolf and Cal take turns drinking from the jar. It's over half empty by the time the rest of the team make their way to the tents. The jar is capped, left next to Cal's seat as the two sit next to the fire, staring into the dying flames. The moonshine makes them both warm and fuzzy, bordering on drunk.

Cal stands, swaying slightly, before she starts to walk across camp toward their tent. Wolf follows her, wanting to make sure she gets to bed safely. Cal steps through the door, with him close on her heels. She removes the gun belt, sliding it under the cot, which she glares at. She grabs her bedding, pulling it to the floor. Then, not caring about Wolf's roving gaze, strips out of her hiking clothes and changes into pajamas. Wolf can't help but smile at her. He pulls his bedding to the floor and grabs a couple of bottles of water from his backpack, setting one next to Cal's pillow. She climbs into her bedding and Wolf into his.

"I'm not sure if this is a good idea," Cal faces Wolf, blinking to try to clear her vision.

"What? The trip or us drinking?" Wolf hesitantly brushes a strand of hair from her eyes.

"Yes," Cal smirks, sliding closer to him. "We were always good at this..." she motions vaguely before leaning in and pressing her lips to his. Wolf pushes her back only long enough to shut the lanterns off.

Chapter 9

Cal and Wolf lay in their tent, listening to the sounds of the camp outside their tent. The desert breeze brings with it smells of the fire, and what may be pancakes. Cal is almost sure she smells pancakes. She moves slightly, snuggling closer to Wolf. She lies on her side, his arms wrapped around her and her head on his chest, listening to his heartbeat.

"Morning," Wolf mutters,

"Morning," Cal replies.

"How are ya feeling? Any regrets?" Wolf asks, looking down at her.

"I'm fine. Why regret anything?" She laughs, motioning from his naked form to hers. "This we have down to a science." Cal pulls away from him, letting the blankets fall away from her as she stands. She gets dressed. Wolf rolls onto his side to watch her. "It was everything else we were bad at," she says as she picks up the water bottle, glad to see it's been partially drank already. At least drunk Cal hadn't made all the bad decisions the night before. She opens it, taking a long drink, not sure if the twisting in her gut is guilt or too much moonshine. Sitting on her cot, Cal pulls on her boots.

"That we can agree on," he nods, sitting up. This morning, he finally got a good look at her tattoo. "I like the ink. When did you get it done?"

"About three months ago," Cal says as she steps from the tent. She squints at the sunlight, muttering to herself as she closes the tent door. Wolf watches her leave, then gets ready for the day himself. She makes a mental note to yell at Brock the next time she sees him. As much as Cal loves the moonshine, she can't trust herself while drinking it any more. She joins the others sitting at the fire, taking the offered cup of coffee. She sips it, staring off toward the horizon. Tessa offers her a plate of pancakes, which she accepts. Nibbling on a dry pancake and drinking her coffee, she listens as Bowen explains the logistics of going down into the well. He had seen a room down there but isn't sure how big it is.

Cal plans to pack a couple of the high-powered flashlights she had brought with her. Finishing her light breakfast, Cal tosses her plate in the fire and sets her empty mug aside before she makes her way back toward her tent. Nausea rolls through her, making Cal pause while she tries to figure out if she has to vomit or not. She isn't sure if it's the moonshine, food and coffee or last night's events. Once the feeling subsides, she opens the tent flap and steps inside. Cal is mildly surprised to see Wolf sitting on his cot, drinking water and snacking on plain granola.

Her bag is set on the cot, she makes sure her headlamp is packed, as well as the two high-powered flashlights and a few smaller LED lights. She fastens her gun belt around her waist, then shoulders her bag. She turns to find Wolf kneeling behind her, smiling that damn predatory smile. Her heart double times against her ribs with their physical proximity, and her gut twists with guilt. Wolf steps aside to let her pass.

"Should we clean this up before we go?" He asks, patting the blankets in a way that seems more like an invitation to join him in those covers than to clean up their bedding.

"We can take care of that tonight. You're still a bed hog," Cal says as she strides out of the tent and into camp.

Wolf watches her go, shaking his head. He knows she's right. The physical part they were good at, and always would be. The emotional stuff was harder for them. Wolf takes it upon himself to separate their bedding and toss it on each cot before he grabs his headlamp, water bottle, and shoulder holster, then follows her lead out into the camp. He is the last one getting ready. Wolf sets his things down, shrugs his shoulder holster into place, then clips both his headlamp and his water bottle to his belt loops.

Cal leads them out into the desert after a brief pause at the oasis to top off and refill water. Once inside the tomb, she heads directly for the room with the well. There is no need to linger or delay the climb. She wants to get as much exploring done as they can during this trip. Once in the well room, Bowen is the first one on the ropes, after turning on his headlamp, he drops over the side and works his way down the wall. While he climbs, everyone else gets the climbing harnesses on.

Bowen yells up sometime later. His words are distorted as they echo up the stone tunnel, but they sound positive. Cal shoulders her bag, clips herself to the ropes, steps up onto the well's wall. She offers a small wave and wink to the team before dropping over the side. It's a long climb down, much longer than Cal had been expecting. She drops to the ground, soft sand puffing up around her. This process repeats as each person descends into the well and joins their coworkers and boss.

The room is dark, too dark for just their headlamps to penetrate. Cal sets her bag down, pulling out the flashlights she brought to the tomb with her. Keeping one high-powered light with her, she hands the other to Wolf. Everyone else gets bright LED lights before she closes the bag and swings it back onto her shoulders again. The small group spread out in the large open space, making sure they are in sight of at least the person to their left and right. They sweep through the room, looking for a wall or doorway of any kind. The team does eventually find a wall with a large archway that just opens into blackness. Cal and Wolf lead their small team through the arch, slowing their pace considerably to keep an eye out for traps. The walls in this part are smooth, with the occasional niche. Cal carefully steps forward, shining her light into one of these openings.

She chuckles, mildly surprised to see a skull staring back at her. Cal is not sure if all the openings hold skulls. A stifled scream from the other side of the hall causes her to turn around. Tessa has also decided to peek in one of the openings. The redhead scrambles backward, falling into Wolf's arms as he turns to check on their medic.

"It's just a skull. We all have one." Cal says, unsympathetically.

"I know. Just not used to seeing them in the walls," Tessa says as she pulls herself from Wolf. She smooths her hands over her hair, stepping away from the bodyguard and continuing the walk down the wall. Cal chuckles, leading the way further into the dark abyss. The high-power lamps help cut through the darkness, but the rest of the lights do little to help illuminate the space ahead of them. Cal stops suddenly.

"Hold up," she says firmly causing the team to stop. Wolf walks over to her, his light illuminating a thin wire strung across the room. "We're getting close to something," Cal mutters as she ducks under the wire. She sets her backpack down, rummaging in the pockets for a few moments before she finds a roll of bright yellow marking tape. She pulls a length off, tying it around the wire before tearing off several lengths of the ribbon, which she hands to the others as they cautiously approach. The strands are tied at random intervals along the length of the wire. Everyone follows her under the wire as she drops the marking tape back into her bag and shoulders her pack. They follow her hesitantly into the darkness, not wanting to be decapitated if the next trap is missed.

The rest of the hike seems to be made of endless limestone and dirt. They stop, turning to look back the way they have come. Cal looks in the direction they had been walking before looking at Wolf.

"I don't think we're going to find anything down here. It just seems to keep going. She says, looking from one person to the next. While traps meant artifacts or treasure, they also meant misdirection. Traps and long plain hallways could lead to nowhere. Those ideas echoed in her brain as she tried to pull herself away from those negative thoughts.

"We might as well head back. There are a few other tunnels to explore," Wolf says, stifling a quiet yawn. With a murmured agreement, the whole team turns, walking back the way they had come. They are walking only slightly faster, keeping an eye out for the yellow ribbons. Someone's stomach growls, echoing in the empty hallway. Cal turns, looking at a slightly embarrassed Wolf.

"Work up an appetite with the hike or last night?" Tessa says coolly. Cal covers her mouth, stifling laughter. She walks ahead, ignoring the glare from the medic.

"Definitely last night. This was easy," Wolf grins, not even bothering to hide what happened with him and Cal, after all, they're adults and what happens in their tent is their business. Tessa blushes a faint pink, either out of anger or embarrassment. No one is sure which. She moves to walk along with Cy and put distance between herself and the two leaders.

"I think you hurt her feelings," Cal mutters, picking up the pace just a little bit. She wants to get out of this well. Out of the darkness. Something doesn't feel right.

"Feels like China," Wolf remarks, only partially using it to change the subject. Cal glances at him and nods.

"Yeah. I don't like that. We know how that ended," she mutters.

"Not my fault," Wolf shrugs.

"Not mine either. Your job is to keep the team safe, which means making sure the locals don't revolt," Cal points out.

"You're supposed to vet the help. Not me," Wolf shoots back, glaring at her.

Cal waves him off, ducking under the wire again. The team fans out in the hallway, leaving only headlamps and flashlights to pinpoint where each person is. Cal doesn't worry about bringing them back together, after all, it's a safe walk. Once back under the well, Bowen leads the team up the opening, followed by Cal, Cy, Tessa, and Wolf.

"Let's sit and eat before we finish exploring for the day," Cal says, sitting on the ground with her legs crossed and her bag next to her. Everyone else takes seats in the sand, pulling jerky and trail mix from their bags. Quiet conversation starts as they eat. Wolf watches Cal while half-listening to Bowen and Cy.

"Do you always have more than one lady on the hook?" It's Tessa's voice that pulls his attention away from Cal. Wolf looks at her, not surprised. Tessa is cute, and if he wasn't in the complicated mess he was in right now, Wolf would be interested in at least a physical encounter with the medic.

"Eh. Sometimes it happens," he shrugs.

"It's a bit rude," Tessa half whines, eating a bit of jerky.

"I'm an unattached red-blooded male. I don't have to be committed to anyone," he shrugs.

Tessa rolls her eyes and turns slightly away from him. Their conversation has grabbed Cal's attention. She watches, her head tipped slightly to one side as she chews thoughtfully.

Cal pulls herself to her feet, wincing as her knee pops loudly. Wolf turns to look at her. She waves him off. Everyone else stands, dusting themselves off. Cal leads the way toward the room of hallways. The team has gone silent and tense. She doesn't like this, something feels off. It could just be exhaustion, or it could mean trouble. Cal leads them down the third hallway, the only other safe one. She could be on her own for all she knows, not bothering to check if her team is following her. Wolf does his job and follows her. Since the rest of the team doesn't dare go exploring on their own, they follow the two into the darkness. Cal keeps the pace slow, limping a bit, with Wolf walking as close to her as he can while not touching her.

"You don't have to be so close," Cal growls.

"Not what you said last night," Wolf pauses and smirks, "or in Australia, France, Ireland, Peru, China or –"

"Shut it," she snaps at him. Her cheeks blush a faint pink, and she is glad the darkness helps hide it. Only Wolf is able to see it. "Last night was a drunk mistake," she adds somewhat hastily. He doesn't need to know it's a mistake she would gladly make again and again.

"Sure," he chuckles.

The rest of the team just listens, not sure if they should step in or let them figure things out on their own. It is safer for the team as well as their leaders. Cal has stabbed Wolf, and here they were arguing, good-natured, about their past.

The hall is long and narrow, just as the others had been. However, this one opens into a room that is lined with even more doorways. Cal finds a flat space surface, pulling the map and pencil from her bag. Setting the flashlight down, she adds the tunnel and the room they're currently in. Nothing is to scale, and she is running out of room on the page. Another headlamp illuminates the paper.

"The tomb is larger than they thought." It's Amir's voice. She looks up at him, nodding her head.

"We're gonna need a bigger map," Wolf smirks, joining the two of them.

"You do realize we're using a coffin as a table, correct?" Amir adds, standing up. Cal lifts the map, looking down at her makeshift table. Sure enough, it's the plain outer box of a sarcophagus.

"Sorry," she says to the box moving off the surface and putting the map away. Tessa, Bowen, and Cy join them around the rectangular box. Amir kneels next to it, brushing away caked-on dirt and dust from the side of the coffin. He runs his fingers over the carved hieroglyphics.

"It's one of the wives," Amir says as he stands.

Cal picks up the flashlight, turning the bright light to the walls and illuminating the murals. Three sides of the tomb seem to depict scenes of the woman's life. The last wall depicts the ankh being handed from her to her husband. The paintings seem to flow around three doors; the one they came out through and two others. Amir makes his way to the pendant painting. He stops next to Cal. Wolf watches the two.

"Correct me if I'm wrong, but our Queen gifted the Pharaoh the pendant. Now the question is, how did she get it," Cal looks over the painting again.

"She may have had it crafted, found it, or purchased it." Amir shrugs. "She may have even bartered for the pendant."

"Bartered what?" Tessa asks, looking around the room. There didn't seem to be many things for this lady to take into the afterlife.

"Any number of things: precious stones, jewelry, animals, herself," Amir says as he turns to look at Tessa. "It all depends on how badly she wanted to get this pendant. However, I said wives. It seems the owner of this tomb had a few."

"A few? At the same time?" Tessa makes a face as if grossed out by that idea.

"Not in this case. From what her tomb says. This one passed away young, and during childbirth. She was his first

wife. I'm sure we'll find the tombs of the others soon enough."
Amir explains, walking back toward the sarcophagus. Cal looks
through a nearby doorway, finding the room caved in. She
moves to another doorway, letting the team talk. Cal finds
another room collapsed.

"I'm not sure how much further we'll get. At least two of
these rooms have collapsed," Cal says, emerging from the
shadows.

"We can't get much further here, we should head back
and check out those other two rooms," Wolf speaks up, looking
over the room. Cal nods, the words having been taken right
out of her mouth.

Cal lets Wolf lead the team back the way they came.

"We'll split up. Watch out for traps and keep your
hands to yourself. That goes double for you, Bowen," Cal says,
she makes her way toward a door with Cy following her. She
glances over her shoulder, watching the rest of her team do the
same. Tessa and Bowen join Amir looking in one of the other
doors. Wolf glances between the two groups. With a shrug, he
joins Cal in her room. She glares at him, then continues her
walk into the room. Wolf falls into step behind her. The rest of
the team are already lost to the shadows as they look for
anything of interest.

"Can we talk about last night?" Wolf asks. He speaks quietly, standing close to her.

"That's the problem, Wolf. You never understood how one-night stands work." Cal chuckles. "Blame Brock's magic elixir. It was a drunk mistake," as she speaks, she looks over the walls and floor. Wolf steps forward, wrapping an arm around her waist. He pulls her close to him, stopping them both in their tracks. Cal blinks, her attention falling to the barbed wire stretched at eyeball height in front of her. Goosebumps racing down her arms. She is keenly aware of his strong arm wrapped around her waist and holding her firmly against him. His hand rests on her hip, just below her gunshot wound. Cal can smell his cologne, gunpowder, and dirt. She shrugs him off, ducking under the wire. Cal pulls the marking tape out of her side pocket and ties a few lengths to the wire.

"You're distracted, just like China," he mutters, following her under the wire.

"The common thread is you, Wolf." She calls over her shoulder as she makes her way further down the hall. Wolf keeps more distance between them, making sure she doesn't get almost killed again. "I can't work with you." The words float back to him, stinging more than they should have. Cal walks along, not keeping as close of an eye on the floor as she should have. Dirt has given way to stones, and not all of them are limestone. Wolf eyes a few odd-looking stones, just as Cal steps down on one.

The stone sinks, causing Cal to stop in her tracks. She immediately drops down, trying to get as flat to the ground as she can. The flashlight she carries bounces off the floor, skittering away. Three large arrows shoot over her head, across the hallway, embedding into the limestone where she had just been standing. Cal lays there, staring up into the darkness and cursing. She sits up and slowly pulls herself to her feet. Cal dusts herself off, limping her way down the path. Wolf catches up to her.

"You ok?" Wolf asks.

"Yeah. Fine." She mutters, taking a moment to look at the scrapes burning on her palm. At her feet, the bright light flickers and dies. Cal sets her bag between her feet, putting the flashlight into it. She swings the bag onto her shoulders, wincing. Falling onto limestone was probably not the best idea, but at least she knows her reflexes still work. Wolf glances at her out of the corner of her eye. She dusts off her shirt, almost absently.

"You sure?" Wolf asks as they walk on. The hall is narrowing now. Cy lingers behind them, taking in any designs in he finds on the walls.

"Yeah, I'm fine. Bruised my ego more than anything else." Cal grumbles, raking her fingers through her hair. They fall into an uncomfortable silence as they walk. The hall narrows further, before coming to a steep staircase. Cal starts down it slowly, not wanting to fall. Wolf waits at the top, looking down at her. Behind them, the rest of the team has slowly trickled down the path, brought forth by the twang of the arrows. Wolf glances from the advancing team down to Cal and back again.

Cal has disappeared into the darkness, leaving Wolf and the others to catch up with her. The stairs have led to another burial room containing two sarcophagi in it. Amir breaks away from the group to look over the limestone coffins. Carefully, he brushes away years of dirt and grime. His lips move as he reads. Cal takes a moment to observe the small room. Aside from the decor on the coffins, the room is plain. There may have been murals here once upon a time, but they are long since gone. Cal finds this odd, with no sunlight or wind, the murals should be bright and noticeable. It's almost as if the paint has been purposefully removed.

"Sons. Twins." Amir speaks as he stands.

"Buried together?" Cal tips her head to one side.

"Died together. The story is somewhat unclear, but since they were born together and died together, their father felt it appropriate they travel to the afterlife together." Amir looks from one coffin to the next and back again. "Their father wanted to keep these brothers close even in the afterlife."

Cal nods, looking around. The room is rectangular, with just the two coffins in the middle. The floor is stone and in one corner, almost as an afterthought, is a small doorway. Cal makes her way over to the opening, shuffling through the door into a short hallway that opens into a large room.

"We have another room!" She calls back down the hallway. Her voice echoes back. One by one, the team squeezes through the doorway and into the room. The space is large and empty. Everyone spreads out, illuminating the room faintly with their lights. The walls are partially painted, but the mural is unfinished. One wall is done in perfect detail, then the others are half painted or sport just outlines.

"This is the start of a larger burial room," Amir says, looking around. "I wonder if the brothers weren't meant to be buried here before their untimely death."

"Or if the whole royal family was going to be moved here," Cal says, standing in front of a section of the mural's outline. It seems to depict several sarcophagi, with a person in each one. Beneath each image is a name cartouche or the start of them.

"I would agree, but none of these is the pharaoh," Amir says as he motions to the walls.

"There can't be much more to this tomb, can there?" Wolf asks. His voice is right over Cal's shoulder, his breath tickling her neck and ear. She spins, glaring at him before pushing past him. She heads back for the small opening that passes as a doorway. Cal squeezes out the door. Wolf waves for them to follow, and they all make their way back through the Twin's Room. Cal leads them back the way they came, up the stairs and back into the Room of Hallways.

"We only have two more halls and then the long path under the well," Cal says to no one in particular. She can feel Wolf lingering behind her. She walks a bit faster, stepping over the odd-shaped stones. The rest of the team follows in her footsteps. It's a miracle no one else has tripped any traps on the way down here. Once they are back in the hallway, she motions towards the last two hallways. "Do we want to split up or check them all out as a team?" She asks.

"I say we stick together, just in case," Wolf says as he moves to stand next to Cal. Everyone nods. Cal leads the way down the hallway, with Wolf following close behind her. Tessa and Amir are next, with Cy and Bowen bringing up the rear. They walk on quietly. The air is tense, mostly due to whatever Wolf and Cal are dealing with or the quiet of the tomb.

The two leaders try to keep the pace slow, not wanting to find any more traps. The hall narrows for a few feet, forcing the team to walk single file before it fans out into a much wider walkway. Dirt gives way to stone, then goes back to dirt, all within a few hundred feet. Cal looks over the walls, trying to find any openings or walkways. She is not at all surprised to just see a wall. Cal thinks about what will happen after this dig. She will go back to New Mexico and put a few thousand miles between her and Wolf, and maybe go visit her grandparents. She has a few things to figure out. The team finds another staircase, which leads to a small room. It's full of small chests and jars. There is barely a walkway between the boxes and jars. Everyone carefully follows Cal, doing their best not to knock anything over.

"All supplies to the afterlife," Amir says, looking around. Cal nods, leading the way out of the room and back up the stairs. They head back down the hall toward the unexplored portion of the tunnel. It's a long, quiet walk. The hallway ends abruptly, bringing the team to a sudden halt. Everyone looks the wall over, feeling for any sort of lever or stone that may trigger a door. They just find a wall. It's almost as if the tunnel wasn't completed. The team turns around and walks back toward the Room of Hallways.

"I think we'll finish tomorrow," she says with a yawn. There is a murmur of agreement and a rumble of someone's stomach. Cal chuckles, realizing she too is hungry. What had been an upbeat walk, is now a slow trudge as they make their way back toward the entrance. The team talks quietly behind their quiet leaders. Amir is telling stories of ancient Egypt while Bowen and Cy compare travel destinations. Cal smiles softly, listening to them.

They emerge into the desert and the sun is low on the horizon. The team trudges through the dirt, through the oasis, and finally back into the camp. Amir is surprised to see that two of his men have returned. He walks over to them, speaking quietly. Cal walks over to her tent, setting her backpack inside. She returns to the canopy and the team, standing between Amir and Wolf.

"They apologize for leaving. They were worried for Selim and his family. They would like to rejoin the expedition," Amir speaks calmly, looking from the men to Cal and back.

"That's fine. We can use the help," Cal says, resting her hand on the butt of one of her pistols.

The men say their thank yous and hurry off to set up their tents. Bowen has gotten a fire going, and everyone is standing around it, enjoying the break from hiking. Wolf casually drapes one arm around Cal's shoulder, a reflex of the past. She tugs her buck knife from her gun belt, swinging toward him. She stops with the point resting against his stomach.

"I told you not to touch me again. This is your last warning. The next time, I will gut you from top to bottom," she growls, pulling the knife away. Cal tucks it back in her belt and strides off toward her tent. Wolf stands there, confused and hurt. He looks down at his stomach, glad to find no holes in his shirt or his stomach. His eyes follow her to the tent, where she rummages for a few moments before Cal walks across the camp to the oasis.

"Aren't you going to follow her?" Amir asks, following Wolf's gaze. Wolf focuses on the desert oasis as though he is trying to stare through the foliage and directly at their boss. Deep inside, Wolf is worried about her. While Cal has always had a quick temper, she has never been this volatile.

"Not sure. She isn't herself, Amir. I mean she stabbed me for comforting her," Wolf shrugs, running his fingers over the wound. Absently he removes the tape and starts to unwrap the gauze which is dirty from the sand and dirt but blood-free. The wrappings are tossed in the fire. Wolf takes a moment to look at the stab wound, which looks clean and like it will heal fine.

"You're her bodyguard, but if you feel she is safe," Amir says before he joins his men. There is something about the tone of his voice that makes Wolf's stomach knot. He looks toward the oasis again. He doesn't remember making a conscious decision, but his feet carry him across the camp and to the water's edge. As he steps through the brush, he sees Cal floating on her back in the smaller pool of cool water. He leans against a tree, watching her. His eyes lock on that little tattoo again. RJC in elegant letters between a simple set of angel wings, all done in black and grays. A perfect way to honor their little man. A splash brings him out of his trance, and he locks eyes with a very angry Cal.

"What the fuck are you doing here?" Cal snaps, crossing her arms over her stomach, wishing she had more coverage.

"Bodyguard, even if you keep threatening me," he replies, feeling tired of this discussion. She stares at him as if she is trying to burn a hole through him.

"Look, I don't need you here, Wolf. Didn't I prove that when I saved your life?" Cal wades a bit closer to the shore, arms shifting to cross over her chest in an attempt to give her some protection from his prying eyes. For once, her naked body is the furthest thing from his mind. She makes sure to keep herself covered from the waist down with the water.

"I'm just doing my job, Cal. Can we not fight?" Wolf says, trying to keep calm but bordering on exasperated. He feels like he's talking to a wall sometimes, after all she is stubborn on her best days.

"It's hard to look at you," she turns her back on him as she speaks. Her voice is cold and sharp. The words come out ruder than she means for them too.

"You think this is easy for me? I love you, Cal. We had something good," Wolf snaps. The words are out before he can stop them. He hopes she either doesn't hear it or ignores them.

"Every time I look at you, I see Rory! I see the boy that I carried. The boy that I never got to meet. The boy that died because of choices I made!" Cal's voice raises, bordering on yelling now. Her hands slam down on the water in closed fists. "I see my son!" She no longer cares about her lack of clothing as she turns to face him. Green eyes are tinged in amber.

"You rubbing that in my face doesn't help!" He gestures to the tattoo.

"Then stop walking up on me naked!" She yells. All of a sudden, the words he had said a few minutes ago sink into her thick skull. Cal wades out of the water as she speaks, "You don't love me, Wolf. Not sure you ever did. Our son died. I was dying and you abandoned me. When I came home, you left me with William, so you could get your damn revenge." Her voice is still cold, but calmer now. "I was willing to give up everything; my career, my passion, my life's work, to stay home and raise my son. I was going to give up everything I loved for our family, but it was all about Bryan's retribution," she dresses as she talks, unable to look at him for fear the tears filling her eyes would spill down her cheeks.

"He is our son," he says quietly, refusing to refer to Rhory in the past tense. She wasn't wrong. He had abandoned her. Wolf stares at her, watching as she lifts the gun belt from the ground. She fastens it around her waist, the weight of the guns is comforting as she storms back to camp.

Wolf doesn't get a chance to say anything else. He follows her back to camp. Wolf watches her storm across to their tent, where she throws back the tent door and disappears inside. Wolf joins the rest of the team, following the smell of food. He sits with the team, taking the offered plate. He eats in silence, his eyes fixed on their tent.

Cal settles onto her cot, sitting cross-legged. In her hands are her journal, a pen, and a jar of Brock's special recipe nestled against her leg. Tonight, she plans to handle these feelings as she always handles them, drinking until she can't feel them. Cal knows it's not the best way to handle it, but it's all she can do. Cal opens her book to what should be a blank page, instead, she finds Wolf's handwriting staring at her. She grabs the page as if to tear it out but stops. A sip is taken from the jar as she reads what he has written.

Cal,

Don't hate me, or kill me, for writing here. It's the only way I know to get you to pay attention and listen. I love you, Cal.

I am sorry. I should have been by your side. We should have been together. I should not have let you dwell in your grief alone.

I was full of anger, and rage. I know you know that, but I need you to understand. It hurts me to look at you as much as I'm sure it hurts you to look at me. I imagine Rhory would have gotten your sense of adventure and lack of self-preservation. He would have been smart like his mom and fearless like me. I miss the son we never got to meet.

I know I don't always express my feelings well, but I am trying now. I need you to know how truly sorry I am. I don't want to do this in writing. I want us to talk, not scream. We need to talk. I need to apologize and not on the page.

I love you, Calamity. I have since Peru. I never stopped loving you. I just forgot how to show you much I loved you while I was lost in my grief. My reasons for my actions are too long and hurtful to write out as a constant reminder for you. Even if we don't talk, please forgive me.

-Bryan

November 20th

It's really hard to hate that man when he does things like leave me apology letters in my journal.

Work first then, Wolf. We are through most of the tomb, we have to be. There is nothing to be found so far, at least none that can be brought out. There is a partially finished burial room, and we have found three coffins. One for a queen and two for twin sons. We also found an only partially completed burial tomb. The murals weren't even done. Name cartouches weren't completed. We have one more hallway to check out, and the rest of wherever that tunnel under the well goes. We have found a few traps. A pit, which I fell into because of course I did. I also set off some arrows, and almost got myself skewered. Bowen pinned himself to a wall with a bolt. Why do riggers always touch things they're not supposed to?

I feel like this whole dig is going to be a bust. We did get two of Amir's men back. They apologized for running off. They are a welcome re-addition to the team, as long as they don't take off again. I don't think we'll find anything. The archaeological find is amazing, and hopefully, the tomb can be dug out before the sands swallow it back up. Amir thinks we'll find more queens, the king had a few.

We're back at it tomorrow and should be done soon if we don't find any other rooms. I think Brock and the other driver, Stan I think, are coming out to help load camp tomorrow or early the next morning, but I could be wrong. I'm ready to go home. I need to get some distance between me and Wolf.

I had a nightmare the other night. I was sitting on the porch in Wyoming, feeling Rhory kicking and moving. There was a warm breeze, and everything just felt perfect. Then I heard gunshots and was laying on the porch in pain, bleeding with no one to help me. I woke up, looking around my tent. I almost woke up Wolf, but he wouldn't care. He didn't care when I was dying, so why would he care when I dreamt about dying?

I stabbed him today. I needed a moment away from everyone, so I was sitting on the cot. He must have seen something I didn't realize was on my face. He sat down next to me and hugged me. I know he was just trying to comfort me, but the last thing I want is to be comforted by the man who abandoned me. I grabbed my pen and stabbed him. He still chased me into the tomb, worried about my safety. William has suggested therapy, and maybe he is right.

Then he came down to the spring, and we fought. No, let me get that right, I yelled. I screamed. I told him I hated to look at him. I hated seeing my son in his smile or the glint in those obsidian-colored eyes. Then I find a note in my journal from him.

I don't know what to do. I'm at a loss. I need to be able to mourn

and grieve, but I don't think I can do that with Wolf around as a

reminder. I still love him, I think, but I can't even begin to deal

with that until I can deal with everything else.

- Cal

Chapter 10

Cal looks at the note he left her again, listening to the quiet conversation coming from the camp. She takes a long drink from the jar, determined to finish the half bottle by herself before bed. The rustle of the tent flap pulls her attention. Cal slams her journal, tucking it away as a familiar shadow falls across the tent floor. Cal looks up, seeing Wolf standing there holding a plate heaped with delicious-smelling food.

"If you're gonna drink yourself numb, can you at least eat first?" Wolf says. He stops, closes his eyes for a second as if resetting his thought process. "I'm sorry. I figured you'd like some dinner, Amir and his men made koshari. It's pretty good." He offers a timid smile, holding the plate out. Local food, especially delicious local food, is a good way to make peace with her usually. Cal takes the offered plate and fork, scooping up some of the dish. She takes a bite, savoring the flavors of pasta, lentils, onions, tomatoes, rice, and garlic. Cal rests the plate in her lap, eating slowly. Wolf glances at the bottle of Brock's special recipe nestled next to her. She glares, daring him to say something else. "Do you need anything else?" He finally asks.

"No. I'm fine," she answers coolly. Cal focuses her attention on the plate of food. Wolf moves, the tent flap rustles again. She looks up, seeing Wolf still standing there. He squares his shoulders, closing the tent flap and turning to face her. "I said I'm fine."

"No, you're not Cal. Neither am I." Wolf says with a sigh. His shoulders slump, and he walks over to the center of the tent. He sits on the floor, crossing his legs and looking up at her. Cal stares down at the man, seeing her sadness reflected in those dark pools of black and brown. "We need to talk. And I mean talk, not yell. Don't tell me we don't," he raises his hand to silence her. "Did you find my note?" he asks, knowing she did.

"Yeah. I almost ripped it out and burned it," she says flatly. It is the same detached tone of voice she had in those days after Rhory's passing. "I don't believe any of it." Cal's focus moves from Wolf's face to the wall of the tent, just over his head.

"Cal," Wolf takes a deep breath and starts again. "Calamity, I meant everything I said. I love you. I love Rhory. What I did was wrong. I was so angry, hurt, and I didn't know how to handle it." Wolf swallows hard. Cal offers him the bottle, which he takes and eagerly drinks the burning liquid. Just a bit of courage for the mercenary. "I didn't know how to handle everything being ripped from me, no ripped from us. You were willing to go against every dream you have ever had to take care of our family and raise our son." Wolf bites back tears as his voice falters. "All I've ever wanted was to have a family. I never thought I'd have that. Then Brock hired me to work for you. I realized I found someone who understood not just my life, but my job. Then Rhory happened, and it was like a dream come true. When you were shot, and Zenaida ran, I held you and prayed to every deity I could think of to save you both." Tears spill down his cheeks as Cal watches him, her eyes now focusing on his face. "I guess it wasn't enough." Wolf scrubs his hands over his face, wiping away the tears.

"You abandoned me, Wolf. In the hospital, you were there, and talking to me when the doctors said I wouldn't make it. It felt like as soon as I woke up, you were gone. I saw you long enough for Brock and William to get me home, then you left again. I needed you. I needed someone to tell me it wasn't *all* my fault. I needed the man I loved to hold me when nightmares caused me to scream myself awake. I needed my husband to tell me we were going to make it," Cal says, still eating slowly. Her voice is flat, almost emotionless.

"I didn't know how to help you. I didn't know how to help myself. I thought if I killed everyone who hurt you, everyone who killed our son, I'd be ok, and we would be ok. I thought getting that revenge would fix me, make me strong enough to look at you again without feeling like a failure. Your bodyguard first, and your husband second. I promised you that. I couldn't keep that promise." Wolf swigs from the jar, handing it to Cal as she holds her hand out. "I am sorry I didn't stay. I'm sorry Cal. I can only say it so many times, even if you don't believe me."

"It's not that easy, Wolf. I wasn't lying when I said I see you, and I can only imagine how he would have looked." She swigs from the bottle, setting what remains of her koshari aside. She moves to the floor, sitting cross-legged in front of him so their legs touch. "What do you want from me? From us?" She asks, turning her gaze from his face to her hands.

"Can we try?" His fingers touch her chin, lifting her face, so he can see those eyes again. "I don't mean to fix our marriage. Not now. But can we at least try to be friends? To support each other in the loss of our child?" As he speaks, he drops his hand away and takes the jar from her. He sets it to one side, away from them. "We both lost someone we love, Cal, and we shouldn't fight over who loved him more. We should lean on each other. Support each other. Not stab each other," he offers a small smile, trying to lighten the mood despite the fresh tears welling up in his eyes.

"I can't promise anything, Wolf. I can't. I want to try, but..." her voice trails away.

"All I'm asking is you try." Wolf shakes his head, "no, I'm asking we try. We both did this. This is not a burden only you should carry. I should have never laid blame on you, dear." He holds his arms open, offering her a hug instead of just taking one. Cal moves, falling into his arms. She buries her face against his chest as his arms wrap around her, and he pulls her into his lap. Cal cries into his chest. Wolf buries his face in her hair, his tears dampening the strands and dripping onto her shirt.

Their tears cease, and they just hold each other, as they should have in those nights following Rhory's death. Neither of them speaks, they just sit together, letting their mere existence in the same space be the beginning of mending the bridges they had both burned. Cal isn't sure how much time has passed when they finally separate. The air is cool, and laughter reaches them from the fire.

"Should we join them?" Wolf asks, his voice hoarse.

Cal just shrugs. She leans over, grabbing the jar of moonshine. She stands, making her way to the far side of the tent where she had flung the lid. After all, she had planned to drink every last drop. The lid is screwed back on before she tucks the moonshine under her cot. "We can. I'm sure rumors are flying about us," she says with a sad chuckle, as she wipes the remaining tears from her eyes.

"Since when do you care?" Wolf asks as he stands. Cal turns, wrapping her arms around his waist and hugging him. She rests her head against his chest.

"Never," she says with a small smile that blooms into a full grin as Wolf wraps his arms around her again and kisses the top of her head.

"Let's go socialize with our team," Wolf says quietly, but doesn't make a move. He is going to enjoy it. Cal is the one who pulls away. Wolf opens the tent flap, holding it for her as she stuffs her feet into untied boots and grabs the plate, then leaves the tent. He follows, closing their tent. They take their seats around the fire, getting a few sideways glances from their team, but no one says anything to the two. The conversation stays light, mostly on hobbies and future jobs. They talk about their friends, families, and pets. Cal thanks the team for the food, dumping the paper plate into the fire before tossing the fork with the others. She listens for a bit, exhausted from all the emotions. She yawns, stretching.

"Why don't you go to bed, boss? We'll take care of the fire," Wolf says, patting her shoulder. Tessa and the others tense, waiting to see if Cal is going to hit the man or not.

"Good idea. We have an early day tomorrow," she says as she stands. Cal walks across the camp, the team staring after her.

"Did she finally just snap?" Tessa asks.

"Is she alright, Wolf? We did hear yelling earlier." Amir says. They all sound concerned. Cal glances over her shoulder at them before she slips into the tent.

"No, we just got something out in the open," Wolf says, trying to assure them.

Cal busies herself rearranging her side of the tent. Cal changes into lightweight cotton shorts and a tank top. She takes a few minutes to finish her journal entry, then slips under her blanket. It's not long before she is in a deep and dreamless sleep.

The team talks and laughs until the fire is burned to embers, then they file off to their tents. Wolf slips through the flap to their tent, doing his best not to wake her up. He watches her for a moment, curled up on her side with her back to the door. Closing the tent up, he changes into his pajamas then slips under his blankets and drifts off to sleep himself.

Sometime during the night, Cal wakes up. She shifts trying to get comfortable on the cot. She looks over at Wolf, who is sleeping soundly while facing the door of the tent. His breathing is slow and steady. It brings a sense of safety to Cal, as it had not only on this dig, but in all the rest of their time together. She snuggles back down into the blankets, watching him sleep. Even in the lowlights of the tent, she can see his holster within Wolf's reach. The feeling in the tent is no longer tense and uncomfortable, but it is calm and peaceful.

She watches him sleep and listens to the sounds of the desert until she lulls herself back to sleep.

November 20th

He brought me dinner. Koshari, which was delicious. I thought he was going to leave and just let me sulk and stew in my hatred of myself, but he didn't.

He sat on the floor of the tent and told me we're going to talk and not yell. We did talk. We got everything out in the open we needed to. Well, almost everything. He apologized for abandoning me. He apologized for not talking to me about everything earlier. He said he felt that if he hurt the people who hurt me and killed Rhory, it would fix everything. He told me he loved me. No, he says he loves me. I couldn't say it back, even if I do love him. I don't think he expected me to say it back.

I couldn't tell the man who left me as I was fighting to survive, I still love him. I couldn't make the words come out of my mouth. He still refers to Rhory in the present tense, as if that will bring him back to us. I know he is trying to keep his memory alive, but neither of us will forget our little man. He is right. We should rely on each other in this grief. We both lost a loved one, someone who was just as much me as him. We agreed to try not to fight. We agreed to try to do more talking and less yelling. We agreed to do what is right for Rhory's memory. We are on our way to at least being friends again.

He held me. No, we held each other as we cried. He reminded me we need to do this together. We both lost someone we love, and it shouldn't weigh on just me or on just him. I am exhausted now. I am going to sleep. Tomorrow will be here soon.

-Cal

Chapter 11

Cal is the first one up and already dressed to head for the tomb. She gets the fire roaring and has coffee brewing before she sits next to it with her elbows on her knees. She is ready for another day of exploring, but is also eager to get home. Cal is sore from sleeping on the cot, but the sand of the ground would have been worse. Wolf emerges from their tent, dressed to work already, joining her at the fire. She grabs a mug, fills it with coffee, and hands it over to him before she fills a coffee for herself. The two sit in silence. It's a later start than normal, but Cal feels like the whole team needs a bit of a break.

"So did I earn my spot back on the payroll?" Wolf says with a smile.

"Isn't that going to be hard, what with dating and all?" Cal smirks, sipping her coffee. She can only imagine the fight that would ensue when Wolf explains that his boss is his ex-wife.

"Would have to date for that to be an issue," Wolf rolls his eyes at her.

"Ok, hard with all those one-night stands then," she shrugs.

"You're the one who keeps telling me I don't understand how those works," he says with a bark of laughter

"You don't. And after the other night, I remember one of the reasons I kept you around," Cal laughs, winking at him. Wolf chuckles.

"If that's what it takes to get some work," he shrugs. The two laugh. It feels good to laugh. It's the first step in being something like friends again.

"Yeah, I think I'll rehire you. Best bodyguard I've had," she says. Wolf opens his mouth to speak, but she cuts him off, "Other than Brock."

Amir and his men join them. Amir is glad to hear laughter. The three of them talk quietly among themselves. The rest of the team files out to the fire, bringing their backpacks with them. Everyone drinks their coffee and eats whatever they grab for breakfast. Once the meal is done, the fire is put out and everyone shoulders their bags. Cal leads the way to the oasis, pausing for water bottle refills, before they continue their way to the tomb. Once they are through the opening, Cal leads the way quickly through their next destination. Back in the Room of Hallways, she leads them down one of the not-so-safe hallways. She scurries under the boulder, hoping her team follows her haste. The team talks quietly as they walk through the hallway. Wolf and Cal keep an eye on the floor and walls, especially when the path goes from dirt to stone. The walls are decorated with more hieroglyphics and murals. They pause at random so Amir or one of his men can translate a section of the wall.

The hall dips downward and curves in a big sweeping motion. At the end of the hall is a long, narrow set of stairs. Wolf leads the way down the stairs this time. Cal and the others follow closely behind him. The stairs open into another large room filled with boxes and jars. The team fans out, looking the room over. Cal makes her way across the room to the far wall. Wolf walks with her. As they look over the walls, they dust off images from time to time.

"About our conversation last night," Wolf says quietly. Cal tenses next to him.

"What about it?" She asks, taking interest in a painting of a man next to a river.

"I meant every word. It wasn't just the liquid courage." Wolf smiles some as he dusts off a painting of the eye of Horus. He winces as some of the paint flakes away. Glancing at Cal, he catches her glaring.

"Good to know. I'm sorry, well, everything that has happened since the concert," she says as she steps back and takes a photo of the mural with her phone. "Try not to destroy anything," she comments to Wolf.

"From this depiction and the inscriptions, I'd say we're close," Amir interrupts the quiet conversation. "They did a good job to hide the ankh, however. We will want to look for any hidden passages." Amir nods as he speaks.

"I agree. I'd hate to miss it because we're in a hurry." Cal says, making sure the whole group hears her. Cal moves along the wall, an octagonal stone catching her attention. She touches it, watching as it sinks into the wall. She freezes, listening for any hint of what terror is coming. The rest of the team is distracted, looking for trapped doors as a small section of the wall swings open in front of her, revealing a small chamber. Cal hesitantly steps through the door and into a space full of sparkling jewelry and art illuminated in her headlamp. Wolf jogs after her as she disappears into the room, sliding to a stop just inside the door.

He watches as she looks over the statues and jewelry. Gold and gemstones would be tempting to any other person in the world. In her hands she holds an onyx, limestone, and gold statue of Anubis, turning it over. She sets it down in order to set her backpack down at her feet. Cal lifts the Anubis statue and settles it into the backpack. She does the same with a carving of Horus and, lastly, one of Thoth. Wolf watches as Cal looks at each statue with the same excitement of a child with a new toy. They are the only things she takes, with a mumbled thank you to the tomb's occupants before she shoulders her bag. The straps are adjusted to better distribute the weight before Cal walks out of the room. Wolf finds two loose stones, a piece of amethyst and a piece of obsidian, which he pockets before following her out of the room. Cal turns, confused to see Wolf following her out of the room. He smiles at her, and she blushes.

Cal touches the stone again, and the door swings shut with an echoing thud. The rest of the team turns. Cal just shrugs, then leads the way to the other end of the room. They walk down the hallway, finding another small room with a hallway coming off the left-hand side of it. Cal makes her way across the room, heading toward the hallway. Not bothering to check if the team is following her, she walks into it. Grumbling under his breath, Wolf follows her. She walks along, looking over the walls, which are just smooth limestone.

"You don't have to follow me," Cal mutters.

"Bodyguard," Wolf reminds her, with a laugh.

"This isn't Peru, or China, Wolf. I don't need you right on my heels," Cal sighs as she finds doorways on either side of the hallway. She steps through the door on the right. They head into another burial room, with a large fancily decorated sarcophagus. She walks over to the coffin, looking over the hieroglyphics. With one hand, she dusts away grime and dirt, revealing more hieroglyphics. Cal tries to find the seams for the lid.

"It sure feels like China," Wolf mutters, watching her. She trails her fingers along the edge of the coffin, realizing she can't lift the lid on her own, before making her way across the hall to the other room. She may not need him to protect her, but she does enjoy his company and appreciates how seriously he takes his job even if she gives him shit. The second room has another large coffin, this one also decorated. Cal notices the corner is missing, revealing a gold sarcophagus. Cal uses her phone to take a photo of the stone outer layer and the gold inner layer.

"Find something of interest?" Wolf's voice pulls her attention to the doorway. The sound sends butterflies swirling in her stomach and a chill down her spine. He stands in there, almost filling the narrow space. He is imposing and handsome all at the same time. Cal pulls her attention back to the coffin, trying not to focus on him.

"Yeah, you can see the coffin in this one," Cal mutters, pulling herself to her feet. Her right knee pops, and as she steps forward, the knee buckles. Cal crumbles to the ground. Wolf is by her side in two steps. He helps her to her feet.

"How long has that been happening?" Wolf asks, studying her as she dusts her legs off.

"Since I got shot. When I fell, it did some damage to my knee," she replies, making her way out of the room and into the hallway. Cal strides off down the hall, limping ever so slightly. She needs Amir to translate the hieroglyphics. Wolf keeps close to her as they rejoin the team. The guide, seeing the two emerge from the hallway, makes his way over to them.

"What have you found?" Amir asks, folding his hands in front of him.

"Two more sarcophagi, one with the corner missing on the outer cover. The inside coffin is visible and still intact. It is beautiful." Cal turns, motioning for him to follow. She turns left this time, wanting to show him the damaged one first. Amir moves past her, kneeling next to it and his fingers over the stone.

"Another queen. Likely his last bride. This one died of old age. The inner sarcophagus is likely to be very ornate." Amir says. "I'm sure near here will be a room with lots of supplies for her."

"I wonder where they would be hidden," Cal muses to herself, looking the space over. Cal isn't seeing any hidden doorways of any kind, but what kind of hidden doorway would it be if it was easily spotted. She moves from the coffin to the walls, trailing her fingers over the rough stone as she walks. Cal takes in the feeling of the carvings in the stone, but she finds nothing to distinguish between a door or hidden opening. There are no levers she can find. Wolf and Amir are talking quietly. "The next one is this way," she says before leading the two across the hallway. Amir crosses to the stone tomb, kneeling to look at the resting place.

"Here is a daughter. So, we have found two sons, two queens, and a daughter, but no pharaoh." Amir mutters as he stands.

"He has to be here somewhere," Call looks around the room. "Unless he had his family buried here, and he had himself buried elsewhere." Amir shrugs in response. That practice was only rumored after all and there have been no tombs found with that sort of burial arrangement. The trio walks back to the main room, where the rest of the team is sitting around, snacking on jerky and granola. The group stands and makes their way back toward the room of hallways. Cal looks toward the last door; this one did have a boulder hanging above it. They had gotten through the first one, with no issues, but something about this doorway twisted Cal's gut. She peaks up at the stone again, trying to get an idea of its size. Wolf is watching her and doesn't like what she seems to be planning.

"Don't do it, Cal. You don't want to live up to your name," Wolf says as he joins her at the door, leaning against the wall.

"Don't do what Wolf? I'm not thinking of doing anything," she says with the most innocent smile she can muster. She sets her backpack down next to the doorway, still looking up at the rock. Wolf continues to watch her, his body tense. She turns, walking away from the opening as if changing her mind. Wolf relaxes for just a moment before Cal spins and sprints through the opening. Wolf pushes off the wall, following right on her heels. Behind them, the boulder slams to the ground, filling the hallway with a cloud of dust. Cal and Wolf cough, waving their hands in front of their face in a futile attempt to clear the air. Cal turns, looking at the boulder and shrugging sheepishly.

"Ok, so I didn't think this through," Cal smirks.

"Just like China," Wolf replies with a roll of the eyes.

"Grab my bag. We'll meet you back at camp!" Cal yells, hoping the rest of the team hears her. A muffled affirmation confirms they had, so she turns and starts down the hallway they are in. Wolf follows next to her.

"So, what do we do if we can't get out?" Wolf asks, glancing at her.

"Hopefully we find a way out, otherwise I hope Amir and Cy come back and blast us out," Cal says as if it's the most logical answer in the world. "And not bring this place down on our heads," she adds hastily.

Wolf shakes his head as they walk along, wondering what choices in life saddled him with Cal and her poor decision-making skills. They walk on in silence. Cal rests her hands on the butts of her gun. The hall narrows, causing the two of them to walk shoulder to shoulder. Cal walks faster, so she doesn't have to touch him.

"You shouldn't have followed me," Cal finally says as Wolf moves to walk alongside her in the small space again. She hates when he does that. Cal drops her hands to her side, so as not to elbow her bodyguard as they walk.

"And let you have all the fun?" Wolf says, sarcasm dripping from each word. Cal rolls her eyes as they hike along. Maybe this was a mistake, too late to think about that now. The hallway widens, coming to a large staircase, leading down into another room. They glance at each other before venturing down the stairs, and toward the center of the room. The two adventurers separate to look over the room, taking photos of the artwork and pillars with their phones. All the decoration here matches the rest of the tomb. There is another set of stairs, across from where they entered. Cal climbs up the stairs, leaving Wolf standing in the middle of the room below her.

"I got doors up here!" Cal calls down to him. She looks up at the two large, ornately carved doors at the top of the staircase. *Well, here's the main door,* Cal thinks as she gives a light tug to one of the metal rings. The door barely moves. Wolf joins her, looking over the doors. He grabs the other ring, and they both pull backward. With his help and the weight of the sand on the other side, the doors swing open slowly. Sunlight and sand spill into the room. Cal squeezes around the door, scrambling up the slope of sand and out into the desert.

"Now I understand why they didn't tell me who I was working with. Always getting me into shit like this," he grumbles as he follows her out into the unforgiving heat.

"At least we got out," Cal says as she looks around. She runs her fingers through her hair as she scans the horizon. The sun is low in the sky, but the air is still warm. Wolf mutters to himself as they start walking toward the sunset. From where the camp is pitched, she knows if they hike toward the sunset they should, in theory, find their tents.

"Stuck hiking through the desert, with night coming on, with my ex-wife. I'm going to die," Wolf grumbles.

"You're not going to die, dramatic," she rolls her eyes. They both know once the sun goes down, it can get cold fast. The sun slips lower in the sky, and they don't feel like they are getting any closer to camp. Over a dune, they spot the trees of an oasis and as they get closer, voices reach them. Cal is sure they have found their camp. Who else would be sleeping out here like crazies? The sound of people makes the two walk faster, eager to get back to camp.

"We should go look for them. They have been gone too long." Amir's voice carries to them.

"I'm sure they're fine. Cal and Wolf are both experienced explorers." It's Bowen's voice they hear now. He is basing that opinion on the stories he has heard of the two.

The two explorers walk past the opening to the tomb and through the oasis. They walk around the spring and into the camp. Everyone turns to face them, glad to see their leaders have returned.

"Where have you been?" Amir asks, half lecturing.

"We found the main entrance. We're on the backside of the tomb." Cal says quietly, taking a seat next to the fire. Wolf grabs her an MRE and bottles of water, handing them both off. The adventurers open the water bottles, drinking the water eagerly before they make their dinners. He takes a seat next to Cal.

"Then we should have found the ankh by now," Amir muses. "It should have been at the back of the tomb."

"I think we're missing something, a door or something," Cal states as she mixes her stew.

"We'll just have to take some time to explore those rooms we skipped. We should be able to do that pretty fast," Wolf says, not bothering to check with Cal, who nods as she forks a piece of beef into her mouth. They're very close to the end of this dig and very close to being spread to the far reaches of the world. Cal is ok with that idea.

"What are everyone's plans when they get home? I think I'm going to take a little break, enjoy a staycation," Bowen says with a nod.

"I won't be going home. I'm heading to Canada to help with an indigenous dig site," Tessa shrugs. "After that, taking a vacation to Florida."

"I don't have any plans," Cy admits. "I'll probably start looking for the next job as soon as I am back. What about you two?"

"I'm gonna go visit a friend, then on to the next job," Wolf nods.

"What about you, Cal?" Tessa asks, watching as she finishes her meal and tosses the wrappers into the fire.

"She doesn't take time off," Wolf laughs.

"Actually, I am. I have a fundraiser event coming up, then I may have a small dig," Cal replies as she stands. Long, lazy strides carry her across the camp, and into her tent. The gun belt is taken off and laid on top of her backpack, which someone had been so nice as to set in her tent. She pulls the half-full jar of moonshine out from under her cot and makes her way back to the fire. Wolf smirks as he watches her cross the camp. Cal drops into her seat next to him, opening the jar. She takes a long drink, then offers it to Wolf.

He takes the jar, taking a long drink. The jar makes its rounds, with just Amir's men declining. When the jar is returned to Cal, she eagerly takes it. Another long pull is taken before she holds it to anyone else who may want any. Wolf is the only one to partake again before handing the bottle of clear liquid back to Cal. She takes another swig, smaller this time, before putting the lid back on. She sets it gently in the sand next to her. The air has cooled from the heat of the day, and the moon shines brightly overhead. Cal stands, walking toward the oasis. She just wants a few minutes away from the camp.

Wolf watches her until she is just a faint shadow among the trees. He excuses himself before following her. Quietly, he slips through the trees, doing his best not to make any sounds. He finds her sitting on a rock, eyes staring at the far edge of the water. Since he hasn't taken a bath in a while, he decides now is a good time for a swim. He strips his clothes off. He does his best not to make any noise as he slips into the water.

The water ripples, pulling her attention to his moonlight illuminated figure. She looks over his body, letting her eyes drink in the sight of his well-toned muscles and scars, more scars than he had had when they were married. She watches Wolf splash water on his torso, as he stands with his back partially toward her. He dunks himself under the water, surfacing a few minutes later, now facing Cal.

"Enjoying the show?" He says with a smirk like he didn't know what he was doing.

"You creep on me all the time, it's only fair, right?" she laughs quietly, sitting crossed legged on the flat rock. With no shame, she lets her eyes roam freely over his form. He rolls his eyes as he wades closer now. Cal lets out a long, low whistle as she stands. "I'm heading back to camp."

"Can't handle what you see?" Wolf grins, stretching to show off his form.

"Oh, I can handle it," Cal grins, dusting the back of her shorts off. "But fair is fair. I yelled at you for staring at me naked. So, I'll keep my eyeballs, and everything else to myself." She winks at him before turning and heading back to camp. Wolf watches her disappear through the trees before emerging completely from the water. Wolf stares toward the camp as he starts getting dressed again.

"You can look and touch all you want, Cal." He mutters, running his hands over his hair before he tugs on his boots. He walks back to camp. As he steps through the trees, he finds just Cal sitting at the fire. The rest of the team has gone to bed. He looks out at the tents before sitting across the fire from her. The moonshine jar is held in one hand, resting on her knee. She takes a sip from the bottle, watching the flames. Her eyes turn toward him. The two stare at each other through the dancing flames.

"Did you ever find Zenaida?" Cal asks quietly, before taking another drink of the moonshine.

"No, none of my contacts seem to know where she is," Wolf replies, sadly. "Everyone else is either dead or in jail."

"You won't find her," Cal assures him.

"Really? Why do you say that?" Wolf asks, tipping his head slightly to one side.

"You were right. She was still tied up in drugs when we all got together. I wanted to believe she had changed, and gotten out of that life," Cal shrugs. "Anyway, she got picked up muling for some guy she was dating. As it happens, she and her cellmate got to comparing notes." Cal takes another swig of the liquid courage before she continues. "She was saying no one had found her. The guy trying to kill her was dead, and her former friend wasn't looking. Zenaida was bragging that she would be out soon and wouldn't be held accountable. Her cellmate found out about me, and more importantly, Rhory." Cal's voice cracks and she swallows back tears. "I don't know how she found out, but Zenaida didn't make it out of her jail. She was killed in the yard." She takes another long drink from the bottle, enjoying the burn in her throat.

Wolf swallows hard, moving to sit next to her. He holds his hand out for the jar, which Cal willingly hands over to him.

He takes a long drink before he hands it back. "So, someone got my—our revenge," Wolf mutters.

"Yeah, I'm surprised you hadn't found all of that out," Cal mumbles.

"My skills are good and my network vast, dear. I thought she was just buried deeper than I was looking." Wolf sounds almost defensive.

"Or you're getting rusty," she gives him a gentle push, laughing quietly.

"Am not. Believe me, I can find anyone anywhere," Wolf rolls his eyes at her.

"Riiiight," She laughs. "You must not have wanted to find me then."

"Cal, I wanted to find you and I did," he mutters. She watches him, tipping her head slightly to one side, as if she was trying to figure out if she heard him correctly or not. Cal takes the jar, twisting the lid onto the almost empty container. She stares at the fire, not sure if it's the dancing flames or the booze making her vision blurry. Cal stands, swaying on her feet. Wolf tenses, ready to catch her. When she starts toward their tent, he stands. She staggers across the camp, and Wolf jogs to catch up to his drunk boss.

She leans down to open their tent. Cal gets the door open, stumbling over the edge of the tent as she steps inside.

She turns as she goes down, landing on her ass. Wolf chuckles and Cal swears. She pulls her pillow and sleeping bag onto the floor. She stands, strips out of her filthy hiking clothes, and pulls on lightweight pajamas.

Wolf shuts the tent as she changes, then turns and watches her snuggle down into her blankets. He moves his bedding to the floor, just in case she needs him. He changes into his pajamas and slides into his bed. Wolf moves a bit closer to her.

"Stay on your side of the tent," Cal mumbles. Her voice is thick with sleep and drunkenness. Wolf doesn't move from where he is. Instead, he lays there, listening to her breathing as it deepens and slows as she drifts off to sleep. Wolf lays there listening to her and the noises outside of camp. Cal moves, pulling his attention from the roof of the tent to her. She moves close to him, settling back to sleep curled up with her back pressed to his side. He doesn't move, watching her.

"Goodnight, Cal," he says with a smile before he slips off to sleep himself.

Chapter 12

Early the next morning, Cal wakes up with a pounding headache. She feels Wolf's chest pressed against her back, one of his arms draped over her waist and holding her close. She freezes for a moment as she tries to slowly piece together last night's events. Since they are both still clothed, she is going to assume nothing has happened. Slowly, she pulls away from him, sighing. She doesn't want to leave the bed or his arms. After a quick outfit change into slightly less dusty clothes than the day before, she leaves the tent and makes her way to the fire. Amir already has coffee brewing. One at a time, the rest of the team gathers around the fire. Cal pulls herself a mug of coffee and, seeing Wolf make his way across the camp, pours one for him as well. He takes the cup once it is offered, taking a seat next to Cal.

"Not poisoned, is it?" Wolf asks.

"You just saw me pour it, dumbass," Cal smirks, sipping her coffee. Wolf laughs quietly.

"Ya never know with you," Wolf gives her a playful shove. "How did you sleep?"

"Pretty good. You?" Cal stares at the fire, sipping the hot beverage in her hands. She doesn't know why she is lying to him. Her night has been filled with nightmares of the shooting and dreams of the past again.

"Same," Wolf mutters, taking a sip of his drink. He hadn't slept well either, waking up each time she moved or made a noise.

"We should get ready for today's hike," Cal says, as she finishes her coffee. She sets the mug down, absently dusting off her pants as she walks to the tent.

"What is it with you two? One minute she stabs you and the next you guys are flirting?" Bowen asks, having no tact.

"I don't know, honestly," Wolf says with a shrug. "I'll never figure out what's going on with me and Cal."

"So, this is normal?" The rigger asks.

"Yeah, pretty much," Wolf sips his coffee. "It was like this even when I was married to her."

"She stabbed you when you guys were married?" Tessa seems appalled.

"No, just threatened to," Cal adds as she rejoins the group. "Speaking of, how's the arm?" She shifts the gun belt, ready to hit the trail and get this last day out of the way.

"Pretty good. I'll have Tessa clean it up when we get back," Wolf stands, then makes his way to their tent. Everyone else takes the hint and scrambles to finish their coffee before disappearing into their tents. One of Amir's men puts out the fire. Tessa takes a quick moment to bandage the stab wound to protect it from any dust and dirt. Everyone else gathers at the edge of the camp, and Cal leads them out into the desert.

"Have you two thought about therapy?" Tessa asks somewhat timidly.

"I'm not going to a therapist," Cal says firmly.

"We talked about it very briefly. Not something Cal or I are up for," Wolf shrugs.

"It might help," Tessa comments as they move from the warm desert air into the cooler air of the tomb. They step into the first room they skipped, fanning out to look at the room. There are no obvious switches, so they start dusting off the walls and looking for the less obvious switches. When nothing is found, they move through the next two rooms. The team finds themselves back in the first room they explored. Cal tries to ignore the red-brown stain in the sand as they continue the hunt for any hidden spaces where the ankh could have been stashed. Three rooms and no hidden switches or levers. Cal hopes they find something soon. As she dusts off a section of wall missed during the chaos of that first day, she finds another strangely shaped stone. Pressing it reveals another door that drops into the floor.

Cal steps through the opening. Wolf and the others follow. It leads to a large, ornate room, covered in murals, and filled with containers. She assumes these are more supplies for the afterlife. The team looks over the walls. Cal trails her fingers over the containers, looking at the images. There are only a few they haven't seen in other murals. Tessa finds a small doorway, almost hidden behind a stack of boxes and a slightly offset stone. It's an opening just big enough for a small person to slide through. The medic squeezes through it, followed by the rest of the team. Backpacks have to be left behind for members like Wolf to make it through, but they do.

This room is smaller, dominated by a large sarcophagus in the middle of it. Amir looks over the casket, dusting off the cartouche. His mouth moves as he looks over the top of the lid. He looks around the room, seeing a large mural on the far wall. It depicts the burial in this tomb.

"I think we have found the owner of this tomb. However, the name has been partially defaced," Amir mutters, standing slowly. He walks over the mural, scanning it for any more hints. Cal and the other stand around the coffin, looking down at it. "If the mural and hieroglyphics are correct, the ankh should be in there." Amir motions to the sarcophagus. Cal runs her fingers along the lid, finding the seam where it meets the lip. Each team member finds a spot along the coffin lid, and they all lift in unison. The lid barely comes up enough to slide the stone to the floor.

Everyone leans forward, eyeing the ornate gold coffin inside. It sparkles under the lowlights of their headlamps. Blues and blacks shine against the gold. Cal reaches out, touching the sarcophagus. The metal is cool as she touches the face on the coffin.

"Let's get this thing open," Cal mutters. They reach down, lifting the lid. A musty odor drifts to their noises. It's a smell of decay and old dirt, a smell Cal has come to love. Tessa sneezes. Bowen and Cy scrunch their noses up at the smell. Wolf, Amir, and his men aren't bothered by it. The gold lid is set down on the stone one. The team does their best not to damage anything as they're moving it. Tessa backs away from the linen-wrapped corpse. Injuries and fresh corpses she can handle, but mummified ones have always bothered Tessa despite her chosen profession. Out of morbid curiosity, Bowen and Cy look on. Amir and Cal set about gently feeling the wrappings. There is nothing visible on the outside.

"It should be here," Amir says, sifting through some wrappings near the mummy's head. They find several small trinkets, but not the ankh.

"It must have been moved. The tombs are too clean to have been robbed," Cal says quietly as they resettle the disturbed wrappings. Carefully the team returns the gold lid onto the sarcophagus, then they return the stone lid to its place. Cal dusts her hands off her pants, watching as Amir goes back to reading the wall directly across from the coffin. He dusts off the wall, lips moving as he reads. Cal and Wolf watch him while the rest of the team mills around the room. They are all getting impatient with the delay.

"Find anything?" Cal asks, crossing her arms over her stomach.

"If it was moved, then none of this tells us where it was moved too," Amir stands, gesturing to the wall. Without saying anything else, Cal slips out of the room and back to their backpacks. The rest of the team follows slowly after her, talking quietly among themselves. Cal settles her backpack on her shoulders, looking for anything amiss while ignoring the bloodstain.

Wolf watches her. This is not good. With tunnel vision, she is going to get herself or someone else hurt. Cal walks into another one of the skipped rooms, the last one. A scarab, similar to others they've seen, stands out to the archaeologist. She presses the scarab, freezing as she listens for either a trap or a door as the beetle sinks into the wall. Cal is relieved when a door slides open, revealing a staircase. She jogs down the steps. In her excitement, Cal isn't paying attention. Stumbling over the broken bottom stairs, she rolls across the stone floor, coming to rest against an ornate pillar. She lays there, cussing at herself. Wolf and Tessa make their way down the stairs as Cal pulls herself to her feet.

"Are you ok?" Tessa asks, taking a hesitant step toward Cal.

"Yeah. I'm fine," She mumbles as she dusts herself off.

"You sure?" The medic asks, looking at their leader. Cal just nods as she focuses her attention on the room they just found. The space is almost entirely undecorated, with just a few small boxes. The pillars, the only thing decorated, have hieroglyphics wrapping around them from top to bottom. The rest of the team has joined them. Cal walks over to one of the boxes, carefully lifting the lid. "Maybe we should have gone through all the boxes," she mutters.

"I doubt we would have found it," Amir says to her from across the room. She reaches into the box, carefully lifting out small statues and stones from the box. Cal sets them in the sand. She carefully closes the box, then sets her backpack on the ground next to her. The items are gently tucked into one of the smaller pouches. She leans over, peaking in a box that Wolf has opened. He hands her a statue of Ra and another of Osiris that she tucks into her bag.

"There is no ankh here. At least it's not in this room." Amir says.

"Great," Cal says, rolling her eyes as she settles her backpack onto her shoulders. "I'm not leaving until every inch of this tomb is explored, or we find the ankh, whatever comes first." As she speaks, she walks back toward the stairs.

"Why are so many of these rooms unfinished?" Cy asks from where he and Bowen stand on the stairs.

"The family members most likely died before their tombs were finished, and they wouldn't continue to work after bodies were entombed. It's disrespectful." Amir says as the team gathers at the top of the stairs. Amir's men keep their distance, talking in a language no one but Amir understands. Cal and Wolf lead the team on, making sure Amir and his men are out of earshot.

"I've got a bad feeling," Wolf mutters.

"You're not the only one," Cal replies, glancing over her shoulder as they enter the next room.

"Like China," they say in unison, causing them both to chuckle. It's a nervous sound. Cal thinks back to China, the cave, and the chaos. Two of their crew members remained in the cave, having given their lives for the dig. Another, Sophia, lives in Washington, retired from fieldwork. William had lost his leg. Their guide and his men died between the explosion and ensuing gunfight. She sets her bag at her feet, turning her attention to the wall she and Wolf are exploring.

Cal takes another step; the sand gives way beneath her foot, as a lever slips into the floor. She turns her attention to Wolf. A low rumble causes them both to tense as the floor beneath them gives way to a ramp. Loose sand on limestone sends the two adventurers sliding into the opening, tumbling into a heap at the bottom, with Wolf pinning Cal. She looks up at him, offering a playful smile.

"Mind getting up?" She says. Her cheeks-tinge pink as she blushes.

"Only cause we're working," he stands, then helps her to her feet.

"Wouldn't be the first time." She mutters under her breath as she looks around. Cal is getting sick of falling things in this damn tomb. Wolf grins, thinking back to the catacombs of France. At the top of the ramp, the rest of the team huddles around the opening, watching them. "Stay up there. Bowen, can you anchor us a rope and toss it down? We'll be up in a few minutes." She turns away, walking into the shadows to explore the large room. It's an open space with a few doorways.

Sparing Wolf the quickest glance, she disappears through the first doorway. She knows he will follow her, after all, it's his job to keep her alive. The doorway leads to a small stone-floored room. Starting at the wall nearest the door, Wolf starts wiping off years of dirt and grime from the wall. Cal watches him for a moment before she moves further down the wall to dust off the images. As they work, voices reach them, and those voices are getting closer.

"I thought I told them to stay up there," Cal sighs as the rest of the team comes into the room. She shakes her head and turns her focus back to the wall she is dusting off.

"They're stubborn, like you," Wolf comments as he moves closer to her. She rolls her eyes at him, not that he can see it. "One of these days your eyes are going to stick like that," Wolf chuckles, not needing to see the motion to know she had rolled her eyes.

"Bite me, Wolf," she mutters, brushing past the rest of the team as she leaves the room.

"Would love to," he grumbles under his breath, watching her leave. The team splits up. Bowen, Cy, and one of Amir's men stay with Wolf while Tessa, Amir, and the other guide join Cal. While having the medic with her is a good thing, she is less than excited to see Tessa following her. Cal moves through another doorway, focusing on the room and not the people she is with. Once again, a few boxes are dotting the floor and a couple of small niches carved into the wall. Cal peers into one of the niches, seeing something shiny deep inside. Carefully, Cal reaches into the opening. She lifts out a small gold pendant, a simple eye of Horus on an equally simple gold chain. Cal turns the eye over in her hands.

"Beautiful work," Amir says softly. "A symbol of royalty, good health, and protection."

"Sounds like something I need," Cal smirks, tucking the pendant into her pocket. Amir's man is looking through one of the boxes while Amir looks through another. She watches him, not sure why his mere existence makes her uncomfortable. Cal looks across to Tessa, who gingerly reaches into one of the niches. Cal checks the other openings on the way to see what the medic has found. Tessa holds out a small ankh carved of wood. Cal takes it, turning it over in her hands. "Well, we have both symbols, but not how they're depicted. I swear to the gods if I have to assemble this thing," she mutters, as she walks out of the room. She doesn't bother to wait for the others as she enters the last room. This last room is long and narrow with tables against one wall and boxes lining the others. In the middle is a pile of stone.

Cal dusts off one of the tables, finds the top perfectly smooth, while the legs are carved with animals and leaves. She turns to look at the boxes and moves toward the far end of the room. A glance at the door makes her smile, seeing Wolf standing there. She watches as he crouches at the boxes at the opposite end of her. The two adventurers work in silence, listening to the team milling around out in the main room. Cal tucks the ankh into her pocket and kneels next to open the box closest to her.

They each sift through linen wrappings as they go through the boxes, moving toward each other. While the team talks, she decides to leave them behind tomorrow, after all the drivers should be here to do the pickup. Maybe she'd leave them to pack up camp and come down completely alone. She works better in silence.

"Found something," Wolf turns, handing her another small carved statue of Ra. So far, they have found several figures of the gods, the small ankh, and the eye of Horus, but nothing else. Cal is getting discouraged and annoyed.

"Plans for after this?" Wolf asks quietly as they work through the boxes.

"Just that fundraiser. I may go see my grandparents for a bit. It's been a while since I was out there," Cal glances at him. "You?"

"See the folks for a few days then back to work," Wolf shrugs.

"You're fine with me putting you back on my list?" Cal asks as she moves to the next box.

"Depends on the list," Wolf chuckles, flashing that trademark grin. "Of course, I am Cal. I actually missed working with you."

"Same here," Cal smiles back. The two fall into companionable silence as they finish looking through the last couple of boxes. They stand and wander back into the main room. Everyone is gathered around a section of the wall with a mural on it. The painting is a portrait of the pharaoh, a queen, twin boys, and one daughter. Below it are a few small boxes, which had been shrouded in shadows. Cal sits down in front of the box, lifting the lid of one of them. Nestled in the old linen is a small wooden box. Cal is surprised to see the unsealed wood is still intact. Setting the small box in her lap, she gently lifts the lid. The hinges come undone, causing the lid to fall off in her hand. She sets the lid down gently next to her. The contents sparkle under her headlamp. She reaches in, gently lifting an ornate jeweled necklace. After looking over the necklace for a moment, Cal wraps the necklace in a piece of linen from the box, then stands. She walks over to Wolf, tucking it into his backpack.

The team uses the rope to climb the ramp one by one. Cal takes one last look around. This just leaves whatever is left under well. Cal sighs, getting a sinking feeling. She walks over to her bag, moving the items from her pockets to the pockets on her bag before shouldering it.

"Let's head back for dinner," Cal says, leading the way back toward the hole in the wall. The team hikes across the desert, pausing at the oasis to refill water containers again. Once in camp, everyone spreads out to set their bags in their tents. Cal and Wolf take a moment to separate their bedding and remake their cots before rejoining the team. Another round of freeze-dried dinners is handed around, Cal is glad to see that she got beef stew again.

"When I get home, I'm going to find the first restaurant and eat as much food as I can," Cy mutters.

"I think we can all agree on that," Bowen laughs.

"These things are delicious," Wolf says as he tears open the packaging.

"There is something seriously wrong with you," Tessa mutters as she mixes the stroganoff.

"See, I'm not the only one who thinks you're crazy for enjoying these things," Cal says, eating a bite of beef.

"I thought you liked crazy?" Wolf looks at Cal, jutting his lower lip out in a fake pout. Cal just rolls her eyes and focuses on her meal.

As they had separated their bedding, Cal had been thinking of this trip and the last several months. Even after their talk, she is unsure just how close she wants Wolf to be. Maybe it's guilt from their no-strings-attached drunken hookup, but she isn't sure. Cal quietly excuses herself, taking her dinner and walking to the tent. She sits on her cot, finishing her dinner in peace and quiet. The trash is sat on the floor next to her, then she changes into the cleanest pair of PJs she can find. Returning to her seat on the bed, she pulls out her journal and pen. Cal flips to a blank page, pausing to read Wolf's letter to her before she continues. Once at a blank page, she dates it and writes. She needs to get back into the habit of writing every day. She has been slacking. Cal scribbles furiously for several minutes, trying to get everything on paper. She hears good nights being said and people filing off to their tents. A quiet, tense conversation reaches her. It's in a language she doesn't understand. She closes the journal, sliding it under her cot. Cal is just settling into her blankets when Wolf comes into the tent.

"I don't think we're going to find the ankh," she says to him quietly. "No matter what the information says."

"Since when do you doubt intel? Especially from other archaeologists?" Wolf says as he changes.

"It's just a feeling," Cal mutters as she glances at him. She sits up, pulling out the day's finds. She has to get her focus back on the job.

"A feeling like China or different?" Wolf asks.

"Same, but different," Cal sighs and shakes her head. "I know that makes no sense."

"I think I get it," Wolf says. "The team dynamic has changed, and so has the viability of the information since we have found all these new rooms." He steps toward her to take a peek at the artifact in her hand, causing his shadow to fall over her. She looks up at the shirtless mercenary, fumbling the eye of Horus pendant, and dropping it to the tent floor. "You're distracted too." Wolf kneels, handing her the necklace.

"I told you why that is," Cal says, tucking the necklace back in her bag. Wolf looks up at her from where he is crouched.

"You can't blame this all on me," Wolf chuckles, standing.

"I can, and I do," Cal replies, trying to keep her voice cool and indifferent. *Especially when you're walking around here half-naked,* she thinks as she watches him.

"That's not fair. You were as much at fault there as you are here. You have to take some of the blame," Wolf rolls his eyes, as he climbs into the cot. "Is this distraction why you don't want to work together?"

"Yeah, it gets people hurt or kills them," she narrows her eyes as she speaks.

"So, you're saying whatever feelings you have for me," Wolf pauses, "sorry, *had* for me, means you can't focus on work?"

"I think that goes both ways. You're the one who can't seem to remember we're not even together anymore," she sighs.

"I'm not the one throwing out mixed signals. I don't know if I'm going to wake up to psycho Cal or fun Cal," Wolf says, motioning to the healing stab wound in his arm. "I think I've made it very clear what I want."

"Fuck off, Wolf," she mutters as she pulls her blankets up to her chin.

"Do you feel guilty about the other night?" Wolf asks, quietly, not looking at her. The question seems to come out of nowhere.

"Nah, it was a drunken mistake. Just like the first time in Peru," Cal chuckles.

"That was *not* the first time. The first time was the night I saved your life." Wolf smiles dreamily as he thinks back to that night.

"Should've let the cat maul me. Would've been less painful than what has happened," she rolls over, ending the conversation. Cal falls into a deep and dreamless sleep. Wolf watches her until he slips into a fitful, nightmare-filled sleep.

November 22nd

   We have found a few artifacts, but nothing else. There are
hidden rooms all through the tomb. I am not sure how many we
have missed. Tomorrow we are heading down the well again. I will
text Brock as soon as we are up to let him know to delay pick up
until tomorrow.

   We have found a few pieces of jewelry and a few statues.
Lots of other supplies that we haven't opened. After all, we don't
want to see what thousand or more-year-old food looks like. I
think I wrote about Amir's men rejoining us. Now I am regretting
letting them come back. I understand them not wanting to
socialize with me, or Wolf. After all, I did shoot Selim when he
tried to kill Wolf. Maybe they ignore the others because they don't
speak English. I don't know. Amir seems nice enough, and he is
more than willing to chat with us. The other two, not so much.

   Maybe I am just being paranoid. I haven't exactly had good
luck with locals on recent jobs. Hell, maybe it's too soon for me to
be back to work. Maybe I should have taken a bit longer off. Oh,
well.

   After tomorrow, we're done, regardless of if we find the
ankh or not. There is no point in disturbing this resting place
anymore. We have a few artifacts that can either sell well or the

museums will take. I'm sure it will be fine. Once back in Cairo, I am going to take the longest, hottest shower I can and then go find some food. I am so sick of freeze-dried MREs. I don't understand how Wolf can enjoy those. Speaking of, the tent door is opening. It's either him, or I'm going to be shooting someone else.

-Cal

Chapter 13

Cal is the first one up the next morning, with coffee already brewing. She is dressed comfortably for this last day in the field. A brief text has been sent to Brock to delay their pickup. Cal sits by the fire, sipping from a mug of coffee as the rest of the team gathers for their morning meal. None of them are surprised to see Cal's bag and guns are next to her, ready for the day. The team drink their coffee, grab a quick snack and their bags. Cal fastens her gun belt around her waist, then shoulders her bag. She waits at the edge of the camp, shifting her weight from one foot to the other as she waits. One by one, the team joins her, and they start their familiar hike to the tomb.

For the first time this whole trip, Cal notices that the winds have erased their trail from the day before. The group is quiet this morning. Cal isn't sure if that is due to a lack of sleep or if she missed something during last night's conversation. She isn't going to let it bother her. As long as the work gets done, they can be silent for the rest of the day. Cal leads the way into the tomb and toward the well.

Still silent, each member of the team puts on their harnesses. Bowen is the first over the wall, then Tessa, Cy, Amir, Amir's men, in turn, Wolf, and finally Cal. They remove their harnesses, return them to their bags before they start the walk down the long hall again. They follow their footsteps from earlier in the trip. A low conversation starts, at first it's just Bowen and Cy then Tessa and Amir join in. Cal and Wolf just listen. Their conversation from last night echoed in her head.

She could tell herself she didn't feel guilt, and that wasn't a total lie. She had enjoyed whatever mistakes they had made, but she felt guilty that she enjoyed each and every minute of physical contact with a man who had left her for dead. These thoughts repeat over and over again, accompanied by flashes of their drunken tryst. Cal shakes her head to clear the thoughts.

"You ok?" Wolf asks.

"Yeah, I'm fine." She says coolly. Cal glances at him, then walks faster. They are quickly approaching the marked wire, and she hopes the end of this job. Once at the wire, she ducks under, then moves toward the wall to look for any rooms. She drags her fingers along the stone, still walking quickly. Finding a doorway, she steps into it.

"Hey! Wait up!" Wolf calls after her. She doesn't respond. "What the hell?" He asks from the doorway.

"I'm going to find the ankh, get it to the buyer and get home," Cal says calmly. She doesn't look at him instead, she looks through the room.

"All about you and your treasure. Going to end up just like—" Wolf starts.

"This isn't going to end up like China. I won't let it." Cal snaps at him. She finds a set of stone stairs and starts down them. Wolf and the others follow her into the newly discovered room. They all spread out around the room. It's narrow near the top of the stairs, then opens into a space dotted with more sarcophagi. Jars and boxes are stacked around the room. Bowen kneels to look at one of the jars. His hand closes around the lid, lifting it.

"These are canopic jars. Don't open them!" Amir advises, just a moment too late. Bowen looks into one of them, dry heaving at the sight of a preserved organ. Cal isn't sure which one and isn't going to look, but whatever it is turns the rigger green.

"Could've been a bit quicker on that," he mutters, putting the lid back in place and stepping away from the jar. He retreats to the stairs, not wanting to risk looking in anything else.

Cal moves away from the group, looking through a box on the floor. She finds a small, jeweled scarab, and slips it into her pocket. In another box, Cal finds an uncut garnet. As they look through the room, she finds another small niche, just one oddly placed opening. Cal reaches into it, closing her hand around a pendant. She pulls her hand out and perched on the back of her hand is a small scorpion.

"Looks like you found a new friend," Wolf says, watching as she slowly kneels. Cal tips her hand, trying to urge the creature off and not lose the artifact clutched in her fist.

"Go on, little guy. Please don't sting me," Cal says with a shaking voice. Small scorpions could do more damage than big ones. The creature steps from her hand, onto the sand, and scurries off toward a crack in the wall. Cal watches it go before she stands. Turning her hand over, she finds another eye of Horus pendant staring up at her. Cal sets her backpack at her feet and puts her finds in it. Wolf is looking through a box she had skipped, pulling out a carving of a pharaoh, probably the pharaoh buried here.

"How the hell did I miss that?" Cal mutters, taking it from him. He turns around, and Cal tucks it into his backpack.

"It was in a skipped box," Wolf comments, adjusting his bag after she closes it. The rest of the team is making their way up the stairs, and Wolf turns to follow them. At the base of the stairs, he turns to her. "Coming?" He asks. They stare at each other. Cal admires her normally neat and clean mercenary in all his dusty glory. Wolf has forgotten how good dirt can look on this woman.

"Yeah," she smirks, before following him out of the room. The rest of the team has moved just a short distance down the hall, barely visible in the shadowy tunnel. They're huddled around a door. Once they see Cal and Wolf heading in their direction, they start filing into the space. Cal grabs Wolf's arm, pulling him to a stop. She steps in front of him, standing close.

"Now is not the time, babe," Wolf smirks. Cal rolls her eyes.

"I get a weird feeling from Amir's men," Cal says, looking up at him.

"You're letting past digs color your judgment of the guides," Wolf tries to brush it off. "I mean, they are a bit odd."

"We need to keep an eye on them," Cal says, and Wolf nods his agreement. They scurry over to join their team in a small, empty room. The walls are blank. Cal shrugs and leads them back out into the hallway. They march on, feeling like they have walked all day and, at the same time, not made it anywhere. The team talks and jokes. Amir's men converse together. If they are saying anything that will be a danger to the dig, Amir doesn't seem to let it show on his face. Laughter from the far end of the group brings a bright smile to Cal's face.

"Man, I forgot how pretty that smile is," Wolf says quietly, not meaning to say anything out loud.

"Cut it out, Wolf. Flattery will get you nowhere, hon." She laughs quietly, "but thank you."

"Used to get me everywhere," he grins at her, giving her a gentle push. She rolls her eyes and smirks at him as they walk.

"It may still if you play your cards right," she says offhandedly. Wolf turns to look at her, mildly surprised.

"I didn't think you still felt that way about me," Wolf says quietly as they walk on.

"I don't need to feel anything for you to have uses for you," Cal shrugs. They try to keep the conversation low, knowing how well sound carries in these empty spaces.

"I see how it is. Use me and toss me aside," Wolf says, feigning sadness.

"That's the plan," Cal grins, tipping him a wink to show she is joking. She walks faster now, eager to find the end of this place, if there is an end. The rest of the team, except Amir's two men, keep up with her. They linger behind. The dirt floor gives way to stone, causing the two adventures to slow the pace down. The hallway has narrowed, making it easier to see the walls and the rest of the team. Spotting a doorway up ahead, Cal veers off from the team. She steps through the doorway.

Two steps through it, her foot depresses a stone. She steps forward, an arrow shooting down from the ceiling just missing her bag. Wolf jogs after her, shaking his head.

"Didn't you say you didn't want this to end up like China?" Wolf snaps.

"Yeah, and it won't," Cal says, turning to look at him.

"Shit like that keeps happening, and it's going to," Wolf motions to the arrow sticking out of the floor now. Cal blinks as if she hasn't noticed the trap she had set off. She shrugs and turns back to the job at hand. "Are you trying to die?"

"I feel like people ask me that more frequently than they should," Cal mutters as she brushes off the top of a large stone box.

"Maybe that means you should reconsider how you do things?" Wolf grumbles as he joins her. The rest of the team is waiting in the hallway, not wanting to crowd the small room or potentially set off any more traps. Cal ignores him, trying to pry the lid off the container. The stone is too heavy for the adventurer to lift on her own.

"Hey. Come help me with this," Cal says, motioning toward the lid. Wolf looks at her, smirking. "Please," she adds with a sigh.

Wolf moves to the other side of the box. The two adventurers lift the lid, sliding it to the floor as gently as they can, considering how heavy the stone is. Inside is a nest of paper and linens. Carefully the two of them sift through the packing materials, looking for anything at this point. Finding the box empty, Cal lets out an exasperated sigh. She glances at the walls, her light sweeping over the smooth limestone. There is nothing. Not even stray hieroglyphics. Wolf, must be more patient than his boss, pulls each piece of linen and paper out, folding each piece gently in turn. The box is emptied, and he finds nothing, so he returns the folded pieces to the box. "Come help me get this lid back on." Wolf motions.

"Fine," she mutters, helping him lift the lid back onto the box. The two adventurers walk out of the room, squeezing between the wall and the arrow. They rejoin the team and continue the walk. As they walk, she begins to wonder if she died in LA and her hell was stuck on a never-ending dig with her ex-husband. Cal is not paying attention to the path in front of her, lost in her thoughts. She is yanked to a stop suddenly, causing her to look around.

"You really need to focus, babe," Wolf says. His breath is hot on her ear, sending a chill down her spine. Just a mere inch from her nose is another wire. If Wolf hadn't grabbed her bag and stopped her, she would have walked face-first into it. End of the dig, end of her career, potentially. Wolf pulls the roll of marking ribbon from her bag, handing it to her over her shoulder.

"Sorry, distractions," she replies, taking the roll of ribbon. She tears off lengths for each person, passing them down the line. Each person ties the ribbon around the wire in front of them. Cal leads the way under the wire, continuing down the trail. She is about ready to give up and turn back when the hallway gives way to a fan-shaped set of stairs. The low steps lead to an open room, with nothing but another staircase. This one is steeper, leading up to a platform above their heads. At the top, they can just make out two doors, and two statues of Anubis.

Cal jogs up the stairs, not looking out for traps or wires. She is determined to get to the top. It's the only other place the ankh could be. Heavy footsteps behind her tell Cal that Wolf is on her heels. *Of course, he is, he can't let the boss die,* she thinks. They stop at the top of the platform, each one grabbing a door. They pull and are surprised by how easily the doors open. The two explorers stand in the doorway, shoulder to shoulder, surveying the ornately decorated room filled with boxes and jars around a platform. They avoid the jars, but start looking through the boxes. Amir's men have joined them, beating the rest of the team to the top of the stairs.

Amir and the others hesitate just outside the door. "This looks like the original burial room. I wonder why they moved him," the head guide muses from the door. Cal and Wolf are pulling pendants, jewels, and carved effigies from the boxes. They each get a glance over before they are stuffed in their bags, and they move on to the next box. With each box, the wrappings are replaced before the lid is settled back into place. Amir and the others are looking around outside the doors.

Cal looks at the jars, shaking her head. There is no way she is rummaging in preserved organs. She has done some sketchy things for artifacts, but she draws the line at digging through organs. The ankh is on pretty much every surface of this room, but they can't seem to find it. Cal takes a deep breath, looking around.

"Would they put it in those?" Tessa asks, pointing to the canopic jars.

"Not with actual organs. It would be disrespectful to the dead," Amir says. "As a ruse, maybe. But it would be a jar not used. Are there any duplicate Gods?" he asks, scanning from the door.

"No, that would have been easy." Cal sighs. She walks over to the platform, running her fingers over the stone. There are no other rooms in this tomb to look through, it has to be here. *Unless we missed a trap door or something,* she thinks as she brushes away dust. Cal glances at Wolf, who is watching over her shoulder at the guide behind her. Sparing a glance at the other guide, who is looking through boxes just behind Wolf, she turns her attention back to the platform. On top of it, she feels a small seam. It could be just a crack in the stone, but Cal seriously doubts that.

Wolf watches as Cal pulls her knife from her belt, wedging the end in the crack, and using it to pry the stone up. Wolf moves to stand across from her, sliding his fingers under the opening and pulling it open. Cal sets the knife down, reaching into the dark cubby. She is hoping for the pendant and no scorpions. She feels around, her fingers catching on a chain. Closing her hand into a tight fist, she lifts their treasure from the recesses of the platform. Dangling from her fingers is the gold ankh with the eye of Horus in the middle.

Movement behind Wolf pulls Cal's attention from the find. Behind him, one of Amir's men pulls a large knife from the folds of his clothes. Wolf is staring over Cal's shoulder, although she is sure he is distracted by the glittery gold. His focus is on the man behind Cal, pulling a gun from his robes. Cal fumbles, unholstering with her right hand. She gets the pistol free, firing from the hip past Wolf, who is mimicking her movements from across the platform. There is a flurry of movement in all the wrong directions as gunfire fills the room and the pendant clatters to the ground. The smell of gunpowder fills the space. The two guides slump dead against the walls, leaving limestone and dirt splattered with their blood.

Wolf and Cal also lay on the ground, bleeding. She reaches out, her fingers grasping for the chain. When they find it, she pulls the pendant toward her, holding it tightly. Cal is bleeding from one in the shoulder and one in the side, while Wolf took a round to his side and one through the meaty part of his thigh. He rolls onto his back, cursing under his breath. Tessa runs in, bag in hand, to patch the two up. Bowen and Cy lay on the floor outside, afraid to move. Amir is squatting in the corner, looking over the chaos. Tessa patches the wounds as quickly and as snugly as she can, given their current circumstances and location. Both adventurers are breathing, but it is shallow.

"Bowen. Amir. Get to the surface and tell them we need an emergency crew out here now." She turns her attention to Cy. "Go sit by Cal. We need to keep an eye on them. They're both bleeding pretty bad." She looks at Bowen and Amir, who has not moved. "Go now!" The medic yells, sending the men scrambling down the stairs and toward the exit.

Cy sits next to Cal, checking for a pulse. Even unconscious, she won't give up her treasure. Her hand still grips the chain tightly. Tessa checks Wolf's pulse, moving between the two to check their breathing. The wait feels like forever, and Tessa is sure she is going to watch them die of their stupidity. She removes their holsters, and firearms, tucking them into their backpacks. She retrieves Cal's knife, returning it to its sheath. Voices reach them, sending the medic to the doorway. She is relieved to see Brock and emergency personnel jogging down the path.

The medics set about caring for the two injured explorers. Cal blinks her eyes open as pain rips through her shoulder. She mutters about her pack, which Brock grabs. He also pries the ankh from her hand, tucking it among her other treasures.

"How's Wolf?" That is all she manages before blacking out again. Brock and the remaining team members grab the extra bags and follow the medics out. The wires are gone, cut away by Brock. Carrying Cal and Wolf out is easy until they get the well entrance. The medics double-check they are fastened securely to the boards while Bowen climbs to the top and drops down extra ropes. The well is wide, but not wide enough to pull the boards up flat. They have to be pulled to the top at an angle. Brock climbs up the wall to help Bowen pull the two up. The medics give the go-ahead and one after the other they are hoisted to the top. Wolf is the first, and as he is slid over the wall, the man grumbles and attempts to move.

"How's my wife?" Wolf manages, his words thick and slurred, before he passes out again.

"She is fine," Brock reassures the man before they pull Cal up and over the wall.

Once out of the tomb, Cal and Wolf are loaded onto evacuation helicopters to be sent to Cairo. From there, Brock would arrange to have them transferred to a hospital in the States once they were stable enough to travel. Brock leads the team back toward camp.

"Do you think they'll make it, Tessa?" Cy asks, looking at the medic.

"Yeah. They are going to have some recovery time, but I think they'll be just fine." She nods as she speaks.

"Not the first time Cal has been shot. She's tough," Brock says from the front of the group.

"That is true, but she was closer to civilization the last time," Tessa points out.

"She didn't have a medic on hand the last time. Just me and Wolf," he retorts. Once back at camp, the team fans out to pack up and tear down. Stan, the other driver, is just pulling up to camp when they arrive.

"You're supposed to be ready for pickup," he calls from the window.

"We had a delay. Be ready soon, Stan," Brock calls to the man as he disappears into the shared tent to pack up.

The team packs their gear and pulls down their tents. Brock gathers contact information to pass on to Cal, knowing she would want it just in case. Everyone helps load Cal and Wolf's gear before they load their own and pile into the vehicles. On the way out of the desert, the ride is silent except for one phone call made by Brock. He calls William and Bernd to fill them in on what has happened as soon as he has service. Brock keeps his phone resting on his leg, hoping and praying to anyone who will listen that the hospital doesn't call with bad news.

He is worried about their physical and mental health. This is the last thing the two of them need. Brock is lost in a sea of possibilities as the truck races across the desert and back toward the city. They are still an hour from the pavement and another hour from the city when Brock's phone chirps.

"Yeah?" He answers, trying to keep the worry out of his voice. The silence is thick in the car as Brock listens to the voice on the other end of the line. "Thank you. I'll let the team know." He says as he hangs up. "They are stable and going to make it. The doc says if not for your quick-thinking Tessa, they'd be dead."

The medic blushes as she speaks, "just following my training." Bowen and Cy relax back in their seats, relieved by the news. The rest of the ride is silent as the vehicles pull up to the hotel. Each member of the team says their goodbyes before grabbing their bags. Wolf and Cal's stuff stays packed in the back of Brock's rental as he heads for his own hotel. Once in the parking lot, he takes a moment to rearrange the bags. He tucks the guns in Cal's duffle bag and the ammo in Wolf's before he shoulders Wolf's backpack. He grabs Cal's backpack and his duffle bag in one hand, before he grabs the duffle bag Wolf carries and his overnight bag. The trunk is slammed, he strides into the hotel and get checked in.

The clerk does her best to get him checked in with limited small talk as he waits in line, checking his phone every few minutes for updates. He grabs the key, thanks the lady quietly and rushes off to his room. He knows that he will not get much rest but having a place to sleep was a necessity.

Once in his room, he mulls over why he didn't take Cal's offer of work. The wait for William and Bernd as well as waiting for any updates on the two injured adventurers is driving him mad. Instead of doing anything productive, he beats himself over not being there and Wolf not taking better care of her. His phone buzzes, it's a text from William.

Got a suite at the Sonesta. Bernd and I will meet you at the hospital, the message reads. He grabs the necessities, and heads for the door. Brock takes one last look over the room before he heads for the hospital. The rental is fired up, and Brock is making his way through the busy streets to his friends.

At a stop light, Brock unlocks his cell phone, checking for another update. Nothing. He wasn't sure what he was expecting the doctors to say. As far as the bodyguard knew, the two adventurers were still getting worked on. William is waiting for Brock outside the hospital, wringing his hands together.

"Have there been any updates?" William asks, his voice is tense.

"Not yet. I didn't expect there to be since they're stable now," Brock replies.

"At least they're in good hands," the cook says with a glance at the doors.

Bernd comes across the parking lot, having just gotten their car parked. He may not like the woman, but knows his fiancé and Brock are close to her. They walk up to the main desk, waiting for someone to direct them to their friends. After speaking with a nurse, she directs them to the room.

Bernd joins them as they start the walk to Cal and Wolf's room. As they get closer, they hear raised voices, which is never a good sign in a hospital.

"*You* shot *me*, you asshole!" Cal's voice reaches the three men.

"You shot me *first*, bitch!" Wolf snaps back, glaring at her. Nurses and orderlies are trying to calm the two down, but neither of them is listening.

"I wasn't aiming for you. You moved. It's not my fault you got shot!" Cal growls, attempting to cross her arms, but quickly regrets the motion as both pain and nausea ripped through her body.

"You still shot me!" Wolf snarls.

"You both need to shut up and quit fighting," Brock doesn't raise his voice, but it echoes sternly in the small room. Wolf and Cal turn to the doorway, facing the former bodyguard. He crosses his arms over his chest, watching the two of them from the door. "You're fighting like children."

"Or a married couple," William adds in a vain attempt to lighten the mood. They both glare at William, who steps back to be closer to Bernd. The German drapes one arm around his man's waist, pulling him close. The trio standing near the doorway chuckle.

"There will be no more fighting, or I will let these nice nurses separate the two of you and sedate you both until you are just drooling blobs," Brock says with a smile. There is a muttering from both of them which may be an apology, it's hard to tell.

Outside of some minor bickering, the rest of their stay in the hospital is uneventful. Brock does make it a point to stop by each day and make sure they are not giving the staff any more issues. There ends up being no need to transfer to the archaeologist or her bodyguard our of Cairo. As soon as they are released, Brock, Cal, and Wolf all fly to Boston International Airport. Bernd and William go to Germany, where they had been interrupted while on a vacation.

The two explorers exchange contact information, meaning Cal gives Wolf her new number. They part ways to go to their separate gates when Cal pauses to watch him leave. He stops, as if waiting for her to say something. They both think back to Texas and the first round of "see ya laters" they ever exchanged. Those damn butterflies start-up in the pit of her stomach.

"Hey, Wolf!" She calls him. He turns, smiling at her. She closes the gap between them. Without a word, she leans up and presses a warm kiss to his lips before turning on her heels and heading toward her gate. Wolf stands there, staring after her. He can't stop the smile that spreads slowly across his face.

November 30th

I am on my way home after a short stay in the hospital in Cairo. Wolf shot me. I guess it's revenge for stabbing him.

It's not really what happened.

Amir's men made a move to take the ankh from us, which we found and is in the hands of the Russian. I went to shoot the man behind Wolf when he went to shoot the man behind me. There was a lot of motion, and all of it was in the wrong direction. Both men are dead. I have a bullet wound in my shoulder, which I am lucky didn't do much damage. I took another bullet in the side, but it also missed anything vital. Either Wolf is a terrible shot now, or he was tracking the man behind me better than I thought. I got him in the thigh and the side.

He is fine. We will be back to work in a few weeks. I did give him my new number and kissed him before I left the airport. I still love that man with all my heart, even if he shot me. Brock is supposed to be stopping into Albuquerque in a couple of weeks. I have a fundraiser event to attend. It's a semiformal event, and I hate those. Brock offered to be my date, which I appreciate. It makes attending these events easier. I guess I better go home and make sure my dress still fits. I haven't worn it in a while.

-Cal

Chapter 14

Her hands smooth over the black satin gown again as she looks over herself in the full-length mirror. The bodice is a bit snugger than the last time she wore it, and she realizes she will either need to get it altered or buy a new gown. Cal sighs, raising her lip ever so slightly in disgust at the idea of going to this event. She knows it is good for the museum and good for networking, but it also means being uncomfortable the whole night. She fixes her hair, pinning one side of her hair with an antique silver barrette. The rest of her dirty blond hair tumbles over her shoulders in loose curls. Green eyes stand out against silver and dark grey eyeshadow. Her lips are painted a dark burgundy. For jewelry, she had decided on her dragon pendant, a pair of simple diamond earrings, and her engagement ring and wedding band on her right hand.

She grabs her small black clutch, which sports a black rhinestone skull clasp. Opening the bag, she takes a quick inventory of cash, gum, lipstick, and her ID. She grabs her phone and heels before making her way into the living room. She sets everything down on the coffee table, sliding her feet into the strappy black heels. As she is fastening the ankle straps, her phone buzzes. She picks it up, seeing texts from Brock.

Don't be mad. I have to cancel, reads the first one. **I promise you're not going alone. Your ride will be there right about now,** reads the second one. Cal cusses under her breath as she shoves the phone into her bag. As a last-minute addition, she takes her .380 out of the gun safe and tucks it into her bag. The phone buzzes again. She sees the messages are from Brock, but doesn't answer or read them. Cal grabs her house key, tucking it into her bag as the last thing.

She leaves the apartment, letting the door click shut behind her before she double-checks it's locked. The sun is setting and the lights on the parking lot have clicked on, shining dully. Cal starts down the stairs, then turns onto the sidewalk. She pauses for a moment, seeing someone who is both one of her favorites and the last person she wants to see.

Leaning against the passenger door of his old pickup, wearing a black-on-black suit, stands Wolf. She notices, like hers, his wedding band has migrated to his right hand. The butterflies in her stomach swarm. She looks at him, smiling.

Wolf watches as she starts walking toward him in slow steps. Black satin shines under the yellowed lights. Wolf finds himself falling for her all over again. The only time he can remember her looking this lovely in a dress is on their wedding day.

"I'm going to kill him," Cal says, pulling Wolf out of his thoughts.

"At least you aren't going alone, my dear." Wolf manages, trying to make her feel better. He tries to put a coherent complement together, but they all die before they reach his lips. No words can describe how lovely she looks.

"Let's go," she smirks. Wolf pushes off the truck, pulling the door open for her. He offers her a hand, which she takes. Cal carefully climbs into the cab of the truck. The slit of the gown opens to reveal a bit more leg than she would have liked to her ex-husband. Wolf helps himself to a healthy eyeful as he assists her in tucking the dress into the cab of the truck, then he shuts the door. He walks around to the driver's door and climbs into his seat.

"So, what is this shindig anyway?" Wolf asks as he starts the truck and drives toward the museum of natural history.

"Fundraiser," she says simply, watching the city drift by. They ride along in silence for a few moments before he turns on the radio. There is a bit of static before Wolf finds a local rock station. They ride along, singing quietly with the music. Cal fidgets with the clasp on her bag.

"You look amazing," Wolf tries to ease the tension. The compliment brings a smile to her face. It is simple, but anything more than that would be abnormal for Wolf.

"Thank you. You don't look so bad yourself," Cal smiles at him. "How'd Brock bribe you in a suit? A new gun?" She wants to tell him to turn around, take her back to her place. She wants to tell him how handsome he truly looks, how it reminds her of their wedding day. Cal wants to invite him up to her place to have a couple of beers and just talk. All of these words die at the back of her throat, leaving a bitter taste in their wake.

"All he did was ask," Wolf replies. Brock had asked him; the day Cal had mentioned she needed a date for the event. They both know how much she hates going to dress events, especially by herself. Brock may have used the fact they miss each other to his benefit. Wolf has confided in their friend that he and Cal were trying to work on things. They were at least talking again, which is better than where they were. Wolf never sees them married again, but he wants to try. Cal has confided the same things to her journal. She doesn't trust telling Brock or William these things for fear they end up repeated.

"Sure," Cal rolls her eyes. She shifts in her seat as he pulls into the parking lot. The old pickup looks out of place among all the fancy sports cars and new SUVs. He cuts the engine and jumps from his seat. The driver's door thumps shut before the passenger door squeaks open. He offers his hand to her as she climbs from the cab. She takes his hand, carefully stepping onto the pavement. Once her gown has cleared the truck, he shuts the door behind her. Cal and Wolf walk toward the museum and crowds of rich people looking to donate to a good cause. Their hands drop away from one another, but they still walk close.

Cal's heel catches in a bit of uneven pavement. She stumbles forward, her bag hits the ground and slides away from them. Wolf manages to grab her, saving her from hitting the ground. They stand under the bright LED lights of the parking lot, his arm around her waist with their bodies pressed close. Both of them freeze, unsure what the next move should be. From under his suit jacket, a familiar shape jabs Cal in the hip. She clears her throat quietly, as if to signal Wolf to let her go. He pulls his arm away, making sure she is steady on her feet. He walks forward, picking up her bag.

Surprisingly, the clutch stays shut. Wolf is a bit shocked to feel the weight of the small bag. He holds the bag out to her for the briefest of moments before pulling the bag back to him. Wolf flips the clutch open, deftly finding the hidden pocket. It's unzipped, and he peeks in it before closing the bag up. Cal takes it out of his hand and continues the walk toward the museum.

"Armed at an event like this?" He questions.

"I'm not the only one, Mr. Corrigan," she smirks. "Either that or you *really* like this dress."

"Can't it be both?" Wolf smiles, laughing quietly as he falls into step with her. Music, something classical and played by a string quartet, drifts to them as the doorman pulls the door open. Wolf rests one hand on the small of her back as she steps over the threshold. She doesn't say anything about his hand, enjoying the familiar comfort. He follows closely behind her. The two adventurers delight in an open bar, taking up seats near one end. Cal looks around the large room, normally reserved for kids' events, marveling at the transformation.

The pillars have been decorated in deep reds and bright golds. A dance floor, tables, and chairs have been added. Men and women, all dressed to the nines, mingle around the room. A cold beer is pressed into her hand. Cal turns her attention back to Wolf and the beer. She smiles, closing her hand around the bottle. Cal sips the cold beer, setting her purse on the bar top. Wolf edges a bit closer to her, one arm resting on the bar and holding the beer.

"Dr. Coburn, want me to put that behind the bar for you?" The bartender asks. He is familiar-looking. Cal racks her brain for the young man's name, watching him until his name rises to the surface of her mind.

"Sure Dru. Thanks," she slides her bag to the dark-haired man. He is a regular employee at events run by the museum. They hire the same catering companies, which usually send the same employees to each event. Dru takes the bag, sliding it behind the bar and out of view. Wolf watches the two sipping his beer.

"Besides a fundraiser, why are we here?" Wolf leans close to her, asking quietly.

"They like to have their contributors mingle." Cal reaches up, fidgeting with the dragon pendant. "I'd rather be working."

"We may have to cab it home," Wolf smirks, as they lean against the bar. He motions for the bartender. Cal watches the crowd, seeing a few familiar faces.

"I'll cab it home. You can cab it back to the hotel." She smiles, sipping from the bottle.

"Dr. Coburn!" The voice bellows from the crowd. A man approaches them, dressed in a deep blue suit. Dark hair with silver streaks is combed back from his face. Like Wolf, his eyes are dark. Cal sets the beer down, throwing her arms around him in a hug. The man hugs her back, his hands are a bit low around her waist for Wolf's liking. "I thought Brock was coming with you?" The man asks as they separate.

"Brock canceled. This is Bryan. Brock's replacement." Cal motions to Wolf. "Bryan, meet Dr. Michael Stainton. He is the curator of the museum."

"Nice to meet you, Dr. Stainton," Wolf says, holding his hand out to the man.

"The pleasure is mine." Dr. Stainton shakes Wolf's hand. The two men stand there, eyeing each other, with Cal standing between them. She lifts her beer, taking a drink.

"Looks like lots of potential donors." Cal attempts to make conversation. The main crowd is in the large entryway of the museum, but small groups wander among the rooms and hallways that house the exhibits.

"Yes, there are. There are two people here from Argentina who would very much like to meet you," Michael motions across the room.

"Me? Why?" Cal asks, sipping her beer again.

"Your reputation precedes you, Cal," Michael says. There is something about the smoothness in his voice that makes the hair on the back of Wolf's neck stand up.

"Lead the way," Cal says, seeming to have forgotten about Wolf for the time being.

Wolf watches as the two make their way across the room, Michael's hand resting low on the small of her back.

Wolf chugs down his beer, motioning for another. Even in the crowd, Wolf is doing his best to keep an eye on her. The crowd ebbs and flows between them. Cal's beer is replaced with a wine glass. She laughs at something Michael says. Wolf grabs his second beer and decides to make his way over to the group when he sees Cal shake hands with the two gentlemen Michael had introduced her to.

Wolf watches intently as Cal makes her way back to him. She is struck again by how handsome Wolf looks in his suit. Catching her staring brings a bright smile to his face. Returning to Wolf's side, maybe a bit too close, she hands the still full wine glass over to the bartender.

"Beer, please. Wine is so gross," Cal laughs a bit. Wolf smiles, sipping his beer.

"What did the good doctor want?" Wolf tries to keep his voice neutral and fails.

"Not much. However, his friends hired us to go to Argentina." She replies, sipping her beer.

"Us? Argentina?" Wolf turns slightly toward her, so they can talk business. "What for?"

"Nazi artifacts. They have a small section of bunkers they just discovered and want them checked out. They recently found a huge cache of Nazi artifacts." Cal says with a slight shrug. "Can I get a couple of tequila shots?" She turns her attention to the bartender. The shots are poured and set in front of Cal. She motions to the shot near Wolf. He sighs, lifting the shot. They nod to each other and down the liquid. "And my purse, please." Cal holds her hand out and Dru returns the purse.

"Walk with me, Wolf." She takes her beer and starts toward one of the hallways with her clutch in one hand and beer in the other. Wolf walks alongside her. They are making their way down the gently sloping ramp toward the lower levels of the museum. All around them, people look at displays and read plaques. The two sip their beers as they walk. They talk quietly about work and life.

Their wandering brings them back to the main hall and the crowd. Now the dance floor is fuller as alcohol tells people they can dance. The music is slow, so at least the dancing is mainly shuffling. Wolf and Cal skirt the dance floor, heading for the bar. They set their empties down and order fresh drinks. Cal switches from beers to tequila sunrises. Wolf decides to get a whiskey and coke.

"Looks like we're cabbing it back," Cal mutters, sipping her drink. Wolf nods his agreement. The two watch the dancers in silence as they drink their drinks. They both order a refill, but they don't speak.

"Cabbing back to your place?" Wolf asks, hopefully.

"I'll cab back to my place. You can cab back to the hotel, maybe," she smiles at him. The two finish their drinks in silence. After the drinks are done, Wolf looks from Cal to the dance floor and back. He pushes off the bar stool and holds his hand out to her. Cal shakes her head.

"Let's dance," Wolf says, as he watches her. Cal shakes her head again. She didn't dance when they were together. She wasn't about to do that now. He tips his head slightly to the side, offering her that smile. The smile he knows melts her heart and soul. "I'm just asking for a single dance, Cal. Nothing more." He still holds his hand to her, persistent if nothing else.

"Fine. One dance," she smiles, taking his hand. Wolf leads her out onto the dance floor. He wraps his arms around her waist, pulling her close. She barely resists, draping her arms around his shoulders. Cal rests her head against his chest, closing her eyes. She listens to music as they sway in time to it. She takes a deep breath, smelling bergamot, bourbon, and cedar. The smell of gunpowder and gun oil reaches her nose. For this moment, she lets her mind drift back to better days. Cal lets herself get lost in the music, his cologne, and those memories.

Made in the USA
Middletown, DE
29 October 2023